Framed 2

Brianna Johnson

Copyright © 2017

Published by: Elite Professionals Publishing

All rights reserved.

ISBN: 0692050663
ISBN-13: 978-0692050668

Cover Designer: Creative Ankh

DEDICATION

This book is dedicated to Lieutenant Russell Holthaus with the Simpsonville Police Department, Chief Keith Morton with the Fountain Inn Police Department, and all of the officers at the Fountain Inn Police Department. Thank you all for the help. I couldn't have done this without you.

CHAPTER ONE

Jennifer waited on her last customer to finish looking around. It had been a long day and she was more than ready to get home. She spent all her time at the shop and some days it paid off, others it didn't. She remembered when she bought the shop three years ago. She always loved clothes, fashion, and people. In her small town, people could really use it. It took all her savings to buy the place, but it was something she loved so she was okay with it. Now three years later, she made enough to keep the bills paid and have a little extra cash to save away.

Looking off in the distance, Jennifer began to think of her sister. Tiffany loved fashion just as much as she did. It had been well over six years since she had spoken to Tiffany. Tiffany was the only family that Jennifer had, but they seemed to not care if they had each other or not. Well, could she really blame Tiffany? They had been through so much growing up, but always stuck by each other's sides. From foster care at age twelve to getting their first place together. It was a bad life that finally started to get better until Jennifer messed it up. She couldn't be mad at the fact that Tiffany was mad for what she did, but did she really have to still hate her after six years? Every year Jennifer would call Tiffany on Christmas morning, hoping she would pick up the phone. She would never answer the phone, so Jennifer just left the same message on the machine. Jennifer was determined and wouldn't stop trying. She would make the call again each year until Tiffany picked up the phone.

Jennifer tried to close the shop by nine o'clock every night. She looked at her phone to check the time; it was nine-thirty. The woman seemed to be looking for something so Jenifer decided to give her another five minutes and then tell the woman she was going to have to close. She hadn't ever seen the woman before and Jennifer rarely ever saw new people come in the shop. Regulars loved her store and from time to time she would get a new person, but they were always passing through. Jennifer decided to get the till counted out and put away. If the lady was going to buy something, Jennifer could just get change out of the bag and add it in once she got home.

That night would be the same as any other night. A short walk home to her apartment, sitting on the couch with her cat Missy, and doing the stores paper work from the day's sales would be it. Jennifer thought about how boring her life was. She thought that maybe she should try going on a date or something, but quickly changed her mind. Her friend Alexis tried to set her up weeks prior, but that blew up into a fat ball of nothing. At twenty-seven years old she should have a boyfriend, but no one seemed to strike her in any way that she cared to progress.

Putting the money in the bag and closing the till, Jennifer looked at her clock for the time again. It was nine-forty and time to close up the shop. "Ma'am, I'm sorry but the store is going to have to close. We are open tomorrow from nine am to nine pm if you would like to come back." The woman didn't look at Jennifer. She just walked to the door and left. *Well, that was weird.* Jenifer didn't mean to upset the woman, but it was already forty minutes after closing time. *Oh well.* Jennifer went to the back of the store and grabbed her purse and jacket. It was winter time and in Virginia that meant snow and wind. It was a short walk home, but it didn't take much to make Jennifer cold.

Jennifer cut off the lights and headed to the front door.

Locking the door behind her, she put her keys and phone in her purse. The town was really quiet at that time of night, especially on a Tuesday. She looked around and didn't see a car on the street at all. It was starting to snow again so she hurried along down the sidewalk. There were already a few inches on the ground from the snow storm that came the day before. She was thankful the city kept the sidewalks pretty clean. Folding her arms over each other, she stopped at the light to wait for the hand to signal her to walk. It seemed stupid to stand and wait so she hurried along across the road.

Jennifer could see a street light out not far from where she was. She got a cold chill that ran up her spine and made her shiver. She suddenly had a bad feeling come over her. "Oh, get a grip Jennifer. You watch way too many scary movies." She pulled her arms closer to her body and kept walking. Once at the street light, she heard a strange noise. It was a girl crying while sitting on the ground by a dumpster in the alley way. *How odd.* She almost kept walking but then she wouldn't want someone to do that if it was her. Maybe she was scared like Jennifer. She decided to make sure the girl was okay. Jennifer didn't really want to go down the alley way so she just figured she would yell out to her. "Are you okay over there?" She waited for an answer, but the girl was crying so loud that she couldn't hear Jennifer.

Slowly Jennifer walked down the alley trying to get a better view of the girl. The girl's hood was pulled up over her head and she was sitting with her knees to her chest. Jennifer couldn't get a good look at her face because she had her arms pulling her knees to her. Once she was about a foot away from the stranger she asked her again. "Are you okay?" The girl stopped crying, but didn't move. Jennifer had a strong feeling in her gut to run and she didn't know why. She stood there waiting for the girl to say something or at least move. Suddenly the girl jumped up and shoved Jennifer against the wall. Jennifer hit her head hard on the bricks and almost passed out.

"Who are you and what do you want? If it's money you want, you can have it. It's in my purse. Here, just take it."

Jennifer tried to pull her arm free to hand the girl the purse, but her grip was too tight on Jennifer's arms.

"I don't want your money, bitch!"

The girl's voice was almost hoarse and rough sounding. Before Jennifer could fight back, the girl rammed a knife into Jennifer's leg. Jennifer tried to scream but the girl put her hand over Jennifer's mouth. Jennifer's brain was telling her to fight like hell, but her body was hurting bad. She pushed the girl as hard as she could and lucky for her, the girl stumbled a little. That was Jennifer's chance and she knew it. With her good leg, Jennifer pulled her knee up and rammed it into the girl's stomach. The girl let go of Jennifer just enough that she could run. With every step her leg grew more and more painful. She gave it every ounce of energy she had, but it wasn't enough. The girl caught up with Jennifer and stabbed her in the shoulder. Jennifer fell to the ground. As she laid there she knew it was over, because her body instantly became numb. The girl rolled her over and sat on top of her. Jennifer couldn't say a word. The girl pulled off her hood and smiled down at Jennifer. In one swift move, she jammed the knife into Jennifer's chest. Looking into the stranger's eyes, Jennifer took her last breath.

CHAPTER TWO

Michael walked in the door to the police station. He was running late today. In the four years of working there, he was never late. He had Brittany to blame for being late. She was sick all night with what Michael guessed was a bug of some kind. Michael stayed up all night to make sure she was okay. She promised him she'd go to the doctor when he told her he would stay home. Brittany wasn't the type to get sick so he was worried about her. Michael passed the front desk and waved at Tonya who was filing some papers. He heard people talking in the conference room. Instead of heading to his desk, he stopped by to see what was going on. Michael poked his head in the doorway; everyone stopped talking and looked at him. His partner wasn't in there so he quickly realized that it did not involve him. Michael's chief, Chief Belue sat some papers down and walked to where Michael was.

"I see you're late today. Everything okay?"

Michael just shook his head.

"Sorry for being late. Brittany was up all night sick."

He knew his chief would understand. In the four years he worked there Michael solved more cases then just about all the veteran detectives.

"What's going on?" Michael asked in reference to the meeting.

"A girl was killed last night. I was going to put you and Briggs on it but y'all are handling a case already."

Michael hated when he didn't get a case but then again; he was already working one.

"We should be finishing it up today. We just have to interview the guy one more time. If y'all need some help after that just let me know."

His boss shook his head.

"I'll let you know but we got some prints off the murder weapon so it might be easier then we think."

Michael just nodded his head and walked away. He went to his desk and sat down. It wouldn't take long and his partner would find out he was there. Brigg's was a good partner even though his dad was one of the cops to put him in prison years prior. Briggs' dad was Michael's father-in-law's partner for years. A year after Brittany's father retired, his partner had a massive heart attack. Briggs was just getting done with school and two months after his father's death, he joined police force and became Michael's partner. They hit it off pretty good over the years and have even saved each other's lives a few times. Making jokes on each other seemed to be an everyday thing.

Once Michael reached his desk, he sat at his computer and pulled up the files on the case he was working. The case involved a man in his late fifties who killed his forty-year-old wife for her life insurance policy. It was a really easy case and only took a little interrogation to get the man to talk. Murders didn't happen too often around the small town but, every once in a while one or two would pop up. Michael blamed it on the weather. One day it would be eighty and the next it was snowing.

Michael switched off his computer and went to get some

coffee out of the break room. Briggs was in there hitting on one of the women cops. He reminded Michael of his best friend Mark when it came to women. Mark was settled down and married to Taylor, but when he was single, he was a lady's man for sure. Michael couldn't help but laugh at Briggs. He might have acted like Mark when it came to the ladies but he didn't have the charm like Mark did. He walked past Briggs and poured himself a cup of coffee. Placing a lid on the cup, he tapped Briggs on the shoulder. "When you're ready to go, meet me in the car." Michael heard the girl mumble something but he kept walking. A few minutes later, Briggs was in the passenger seat and they left the station.

Michael had to go down to Brittany's office to give Taylor the last of the paper work. Plus, he wanted to make sure Brittany didn't go to work.

"So, why were you late today, Sims? You're never late."

Michael turned down a side street and headed towards the office.

"Brittany was up all night sick as a dog."

Michael could see Briggs smiling out of the corner of his eye.

"You know what that means, right?"

Oh boy, here go the jokes. "No Briggs, but I'm sure you're going to tell me anyway."

Briggs laughed and patted Michael on the shoulder.

"You might just be a daddy soon."

Michael had taken a sip of his coffee just before Briggs said the words. Michael spit out his coffee all over the dash of the car. Briggs was laughing so hard he almost started crying.

"That was way funnier than I ever thought it would be."

Michael didn't say anything. *Could Brittany really be pregnant? There's no way.* They both wanted kids, but hadn't really talked about it much at all. Plus, Brittany was on birth control.

"Dude, it was a joke. Look, I'm sure it's probably just a virus or something, okay? Don't freak out man."

They rode in silence the rest of the way. Once they reached the office, Michael felt his blood start to boil. Brittany told him she was going to the doctor; apparently she didn't because her car was in the parking lot. He took a breath because maybe she had an appointment set for later that day. Either way, she needed to be home and in the bed. Not here at work risking everyone else of getting sick. He got out of the car and headed to the doors with Briggs hot on his tail.

"Thought you said Brittany was sick, dude?"

Michael opened the door and walked in.

"Trust me if you saw the things I did last night you would know she was sick. She is getting an ear full about being here, too."

Michael didn't even look at Taylor. He just went right down the hall towards Brittany's office. Briggs stayed back to talk to Taylor and Michael went into Brittany's office without even knocking. Brittany was at her desk staring at her laptop. Seeing her there made Michael's blood boil.

"Well, sweetheart, this doesn't look like a doctor's office to me."

Brittany looked up over the laptop and her face went blank. Michael went over and sat on the couch she had in her office.

"Well, I'm feeling better so I don't need to go to the doctor."

Michael didn't like that she was at work. Brittany did look better than she did the night before, but she still had bags under her eyes from lack of sleep.

"Okay, but you need rest Britt. You were up all night, remember?"

Brittany closed her laptop and walked over to where Michael was sitting.

"I'm fine, really. So, what are you doing here? You could have just faxed the papers over to Taylor."

Michael knew that he could have done that, but he had a funny feeling she would be there. Like him, Brittany never missed work for anything.

"I know I could have, but I also knew you wouldn't stay home."

Brittany sighed and sat down next to Michael.

"If I promise to go to the doctor today, will you let this go?"

Michael knew that was about as good as it was going to get. She wouldn't go home no matter how much he bugged her to.

"Okay Britt, just go to the doctor though. No excuses about getting too busy. A promise is a promise."

Brittany nodded and leaned over and kissed his cheek. After saying his goodbyes and giving Brittany the paper work, Michael headed back out to where Briggs was waiting with Taylor.

"Let's go give the old man the news."

Briggs followed behind Michael. They jumped in the car and headed back to the police station. Michael and Briggs pulled back up to the station, walked in, and headed to the cells in the back. Michael wanted to finish up the case and move on to the next one. They arrived at the cell where Timmy Smith, was being held. Briggs pulled out the key and dragged him out. After putting Timmy in the interrogation room and sitting down in front of him, Michael pulled out his pen and began to write down all the information he needed to. Briggs was standing over near the door. Timmy didn't say a word. He just watched Michael write and every now and then he looked over at Briggs. Michael put the pen down and looked at Timmy.

"Well, Timmy, everything is in order and your statement has been sent over to the lawyer's office. They will handle the rest. For now, Briggs will read you your rights and that will be it. Do you need to add anything else?"

Timmy looked up into Michael's eyes and said, "You know, she was a mean lady; a real bitch. I did the world good by getting rid of her."

Michael looked over at Briggs then back at Timmy.

"Well, you might not have liked her much, but she was a human being. That counts for something, especially when it comes to murder Timmy."

Michael stood up and walked to the door. Briggs read Timmy his rights as Michael yelled for one of the cops to come get Timmy. He was getting transferred to the local jail. In a few weeks, Timmy would go to court and be sentenced for murder. Michael and Briggs would have to go to court as well and show proof of everything they had found. Michael didn't mind going to court though because he had done it so much in the past four years that it had become routine.

Walking back to the front of the office, Michael turned

and headed to his desk. Before he could sit down his chief called to him.

"Hey Michael, did you get everything squared away with Timmy Smith?"

Michael turned to face him and said, "Yes sir. He is being taken to the local jail now to await trial. How is the case from this morning going?"

Michael's chief took a drink of the coffee he was holding in his hand.

"It's going okay for now. We are hoping the prints turn out to be someone in the system. We went to notify the family, but she only has a sister. Matthews and Watson are headed over there now to let her know. For now, I'm going to let them handle it so do you mind checking into some cold cases for me?"

Michael nodded and turned to sit at his desk.

"Good. Once you get this stuff with Timmy taken care of, take some of the cold cases home and work from there. With Brittany sick and you tired, it might do you some good to get out of this office for a few days. Don't worry; you'll still get paid for it."

Michael wasn't worried about the pay at all. He just liked to work. In this case, orders were orders. Maybe Michael did need some time out of the office.

"You're right. I should do it while everything is slow. I'll be back in two days or so. Just let me know if anything comes up, okay?"

With that Michael went to work trying to wrap up the case so he could head out. He figured that if he got everything done in time, he could make it to Brittany's doctor's appointment with her. Only one thing stopped him from going to the doctor with Brittany and that was Brittany.

CHAPTER THREE

Michael pulled up to Brittany's office for the second time that day. He looked over in the seat next to him at the box of cold cases. He had a lot of work to do over the next two days but he hoped he could solve at least one of the cases in the box. Briggs was a little upset about being alone for two days but he understood. Michael was only worried about one person understanding him not being at work for two days. He got out of the car and made the walk to the office doors. The conversation he was about to have with Brittany could go one of two ways. One, she would be okay with him going to the doctor and taking time off or two, she could get irritated and not want him to go with her or stay home. He was hoping for the first one.

Passing Taylor, he walked to Brittany's office. He decided to knock on the door that time. After Brittany let him in, she gave him a confused look.

"So, what brings you back in here sir?"

Brittany said with a smile as she sat down at her desk. Her smiled faded in a matter of seconds as she looked at the uncertainty in his face.

"What's wrong, Michael?"

Michael sat down on the couch and looked up at her, smiling.

"Well sweetheart, I am off for the next two days so I get to go to the doctor with you today!"

Brittany's mouth dropped open. Michael sat there staring at her waiting for her to answer him.

"Michael, you never take time off so what's going on and no you're not going to the doctor with me. You know how I am about doctors anyway. Why would you think I would let you go with me?"

He had known she would be that way.

"Britt, things are really slow at the office. Chief Belue knows you're sick, so he just suggested that I take some time off and work from home on some cold cases. Plus, because I know you hate doctors I'm going to support you. Please don't make a big deal out of this, honey."

"Michael, working from home is fine and I understand why you are doing it. I am not sick anymore, but if work is slow then go for it. Also Michael, I know you want to go to the doctor with me but you're not going, so get that out of your head."

She didn't know it yet, but he was going whether she liked it or not.

"I'll be outside waiting for you at your car. I already called and found out what time your appointment is so either we ride together or I meet you there. Oh, and no it's not illegal for them to tell me so don't try to pull that one on me again."

Brittany was pissed, but didn't say a word. After putting her laptop in her bag she grabbed her keys and she headed for her office door. Before she could even open it, Michael grabbed the handle and swung the door open for her. After Brittany made a huffing noise and walked out, Michael followed her. Brittany took her own car and Michael followed her. He figured it would be best considering she was mad. Plus, he wanted to get home after the appointment and start on the cold cases; Brittany would be heading back to work.

The doctor's office was not far from Brittany's office. They pulled up at the office and Michael parked next to Brittany. He jumped out and went to open her door. He hoped she was cooled off a little after the drive over there. Watching Brittany get out of the car with her purse, he could tell she was far from cooled off.

"I just don't get why you think you have to go with me."

Michael almost laughed at how childish Brittany was acting.

"I love you and I want to go with you. We are here so let it go, honey."

Huffing, Brittany stormed off to the office. Michael had to speed walk to keep up with her. Twenty minutes later Michael and Brittany were in a room waiting on the doctor to come in. Michael could tell Brittany hated the doctor's office. Whatever nails Brittany had when they got there were gone. She just kept biting them and looking at the door. Michael almost spoke, but the door to the room opened.

"Mrs. Sims? I'm Doctor Kinsmen. So, what brings you in today?"

Brittany sat up straight and looked over at Michael.

"Well, I was up all night sick to my stomach. I feel much better today but my husband insisted I come in and get checked out."

Brittany gave Michael the evil eye then looked back at the doctor.

"Well, it's a good thing that you came in. It could have just been a twenty-four hour virus, but we will go over some things to be sure. Now, the nurse said your temperature was normal. Did you have a fever last night at all?"

Michael watched Brittany look off into space like she was thinking.

"No, I don't think I did. Could it have been something I ate?"

Michael knew that wasn't it and decided to speak up.

"That couldn't be it, Britt. We ate the same thing and I didn't get sick."

The doctor wrote some things down then looked up at Brittany and asked, "Is there any way you could be pregnant?"

Michael stopped breathing. Brittany's face went a lighter shade of white.

"No! I'm on birth control."

"What form of birth control do you use, Mrs. Sims?"

Brittany looked over at Michael and then back to the doctor.

"I am on the pill. I take it on time every day along with my vitamins."

The doctor started writing again.

"Let's get a test just to be on the safe side, okay? Sometimes, with many women, your hormones fluctuate and that's why they make different forms of birth control pills. Doctors try to give you the kind that best suits your hormones. There is always a chance the pill that you have isn't strong enough for your hormones anymore which can lead to pregnancy. That could be the case with you, but also like I said before it could have just been a virus. When was your last menstrual cycle?"

Brittany looked at the doctor and slowly said, "It's due anytime now."

Michael forgot that he wasn't breathing and let out a big sigh. Brittany didn't move as the doctor walked out of the room. Finally, the nurse came in with a cup for Brittany to pee in. Brittany left the room and Michael began to shake. Looking over to his side there was a table with some magazines on it. He picked one up and read through it hoping it would take his mind off of the situation at hand. Brittany came back in the room and sat back down. Putting the magazine down, Michael looked over at her.

"Britt, are you okay?"

"I don't know yet, Michael."

It didn't take long for the doctor to come back in with some paperwork.

"Well, Mr. and Mrs. Sims, it looks like you are in fact pregnant."

The doctor kept talking about OBGYNs and what steps to take, but Michael was tuned out. He was going to be a dad. He never put much thought into being a dad up to that point. Were they ready to have a kid? He was freaking out until the doctor said his name and got his attention.

"Mr. Sims, are you alright?"

Michael only nodded and looked over at Brittany.

"I know this is a shock to you both, but don't worry. I'm sure you will both be great parents. Now, there is a lot of information in the pamphlets that I gave you, Mrs. Sims.

Look over it and find you a doctor. According to your last menstrual cycle, you are probably only around five weeks."

Brittany was looking at the doctor taking in every bit of information he was saying. Shortly after, Michael and Brittany walked to their cars not saying a word. Michael reached Brittany's car first and opened the door.

Brittany finally spoke, "I'm going to call Taylor and let her know I'm going home for the day. We will talk about this once we get home, okay?"

Michael nodded and watched Brittany start up her car. He got in his car and sat there as Brittany pulled away. His mind wandered around the idea of being a dad. Was Brittany even okay with everything? She did seem pretty upset about it, but then again, he did too. It wasn't even that he was upset, but more of the fact that he was shocked about everything.

***

Tiffany pulled up to her house confused when she saw a sleek, black car parked in her driveway. She parked beside the car and looked around trying to find the person who owned the car. Her eyes finally found two guys standing at her front door. She could tell they were cops from the belts and badges on their sleek outfits. Tiffany's heart started beating fast. Could this be about her office being broken into the week before? She grabbed her purse, placed her phone into her bag, and cut the car off. The two cops turned to face her when she met them at her door.

"Can I help you, gentlemen?"

It was cold out that day, but the men seemed to be sweating under their collars.

"Yes, are you Tiffany Childress?"

Tiffany could feel her body heat up from being nervous.

"Yes, what can I do for you guys?"

The other cop that didn't seem to want to make eye contact decided to finally speak.

"Can we talk more inside, Ms. Childress?"

She nodded and walked between them to unlock the door. She could hear their footsteps not far behind her once she entered her home. Tiffany liked her small home. It was far from what she dreamed of, but it would do. She worked her way through college. School was never easy, but she made sure to buckle down and got through it all. Her challenging work eventually paid off a year ago when she graduated and got a job being a partner at a local veterinarian office. In a year's time, she gained a good bit of patients, made a good name for herself, and saved up a good bit of money to buy the house she lived. She lived in a quiet neighborhood not too far from her job. All the homes that surrounded her were a lot bigger then hers, but it didn't bother her. Tiffany's home was a small, two bedroom one bathroom with a den, dining room, and kitchen. She made do with it in hopes that one day her career would take off and she could afford a bigger home.

"Can I get you two some coffee? I was going to make me a cup."

Both the cops wiped their feet on the floor mat then looked up at Tiffany. The quiet one looked away and the other guy finally spoke.

"That would be great, Ms. Childress."

Tiffany turned to her left, laid her purse down on the dining room table, and walked to the kitchen.

"Feel free to have a seat at the table and I'll be right

back with y'all."

She went to work making the coffee and returned in a few minutes with three steaming cups on a tray with milk and sugar. She sat the tray down, grabbed her cup, and sat across from them.

"I never caught your names, officers."

The quiet one didn't add anything to his cup while the talkative one added both milk and sugar to his cup.

Setting his cup down, the quiet one spoke, "I'm sorry ma'am. My name is Detective Watson and this is Detective Matthews."

Tiffany took another sip of her coffee and looked them both in the eye.

"Is this about the break in that I had last week at my office in town?"

As soon as the sentence left her mouth both the detectives got an instant confused looked on their faces.

"Ma'am, what break in?"

Now, she was confused. If this wasn't about the break in, then what was this about?

"I am a local veterinarian in town and last week someone broke into my office and flipped it upside down. They didn't take anything but I still filed a report just in case. I thought that was what this was about. Now, I'm confused. What's going on?"

Detective Matthews looked her in the eyes before speaking, "Ms. Childress, when is the last time you spoke to your sister Jennifer Childress?"

Why would detectives be asking about Jennifer? What

has she done now? I can't help them because I haven't talked to her in years.

"I'm not sure. It's been a really, long time. It could have been maybe five or six years ago. I'm not really sure. We had a falling out a long time ago and never spoke after that. Jennifer calls every Christmas, but I never pick up the phone. What's going on with her? Is she in some kind of trouble?"

Watson took his turn to talk, "Ms. Childress, your sister was found murdered in a dumpster not far from her store."

Tiffany wondered if she heard them right at first. Her sister was dead?

"I don't understand and I have so many questions. When did this happen? How did this happen? More important, did you find who did it?"

Matthews pushed his cup of coffee to the side and looked down at the table.

"We aren't sure who did it yet. We are waiting for some evidence to come back. We found her early this morning. We believe she was attacked coming home from work last night. We need to ask you a few questions. Do you need a minute?"

Did she need a minute? She wasn't really sure. She had built up so much anger for her sister over the years that she never planned to ever talk to her again.

"No, I'm okay. Go ahead with your questions."

Watson spoke up first, "You said it had been at least five or six years since you spoke last. Can you tell me why?"

Tiffany didn't really want to take a trip down that memory lane again, but it didn't seem she had a choice. The pain began to go to her head and cause it to hurt. It was going to be a really long day.

CHAPTER FOUR

Tiffany thought back to when her life started going wrong. "I don't know where you want me to begin so I'll start from the time I remember all the problems beginning. Jennifer and I were always close growing up. Even though we were two years apart, everyone thought we were twins. We had a good life up until our father died; I was ten and Jennifer was eight. He died in a head on car crash. I was always close to my dad, but Jennifer was closer to our mom. I took his loss harder than Jennifer. Anyway, that is when our life began to really change. Jennifer and I were still close, but our mom started to distance herself from us. She began to drink, sleep all the time, and even forget to pick us up from school from time to time. It was like when she lost our dad, she forgot she ever had us. On my thirteenth birthday, she took me and Jennifer to a friend's house and never came back to pick us up. Jennifer and I were worried that something happened to her. Later that day cops and people from CPS came and took us away. They told us that our mom had packed up her stuff and left town. I'm still not sure if she ever got over dad's death or if she just didn't want us anymore."

Tiffany took a sip of her coffee and looked back at the detectives.

"We stayed in a girl's home for over a year and finally a family decided to foster us. Long story short, we switched foster homes and even got split up a few times, but in the end when I turned eighteen they let me go. I was on the streets for a few months, but I got a job and an apartment. I finally found where my sister was and when she turned eighteen, I took her in with me. I helped Jennifer get a job and finish school. Everything seemed to be getting better. I got into a great college and began my journey to becoming a vet. Jennifer still didn't know what she wanted to do yet or even if she wanted to go to college. Either way she worked a full time job and seemed to be pretty happy. I finally found a guy that swept me off my feet. He understood my past and even welcomed Jennifer as a sister. He was a college teacher in the next town over and even encouraged Jennifer to put some serious thought into going to college. A year later, I was about to be a bride. I had everything planned all the way down to the food. I didn't have many people coming at all. Most were friends from work because we didn't have any family left. It was going to be a simple wedding with my sister walking me down the aisle."

Tiffany could feel the anger boiling up inside her.

"Jennifer was supposed to go with me for my dress fitting one day. I got off work and went to pick her up from our apartment. She must have gotten the days confused because when I got there she wasn't outside waiting. I went up to our floor, unlocked the door, and heard someone moaning. To save you the details, I found my sister in bed with my fiancé. Needless to say I flipped out on them both, packed my bags, and left without another word. I was so mad that my own sister would stoop that low. We were all each other had and we had been through so much in our lives that it hurt badly. I had done so much for her and she repaid me by sleeping with him. I never spoke to her again after that. The last I heard she owned a store on the other side of town and was doing okay. As far as our mother is concerned, I have yet to hear from her and I honestly don't care. Jennifer never really got into any kind of trouble growing up. We were both so frightened by the life we were given that we didn't want to mess it up anymore then it was. I'm not sure how I can be of any help to y'all because I have no idea who she even is involved with now."

Matthews had a pen and paper out that Tiffany hadn't noticed earlier. He must have gotten it out while she was telling her long life story.

"Ms. Childress, we aren't sure who we are dealing with so every detail about her life matters, even things from her past. You said your dad passed away and your mom left. Your dad's name was Jason Childress and your mother's name was Katie Childress, correct?"

"Yes, that's correct."

Matthews jotted some things down and Watson looked over at her.

"One more question, Ms. Childress. Where were you last night between nine and eleven?"

Tiffany was really confused. Why would they want to know where she was at? Did she need an alibi? They couldn't possibly think she had anything to do with her sister's death. Could they?

"I was home last night. I had a late surgery yesterday, but got home around seven. I stayed in the rest of the night and ended up going to bed rather early."

Matthews stood up and Watson followed suit.

"Well, Ms. Childress that's about all the questions we have for now. We might have more come up so please don't make plans to leave town. We also need you to come down to the station and identify the body. You are the only family member that we can find right now. If you decided you don't want to make plans for her burial, then you can turn her over to the county and they will handle her service."

Tiffany knew that she would handle her sister's services. She might have not gotten along with her, but death wasn't something she wished on her sister.

"No I will handle everything. I can come down first thing in the morning, if that's okay."

Matthews nodded and walked towards the door. Tiffany let them out and locked the door behind them. Sitting back down at the table, she began to take in everything that was just said to her. Her sister was now dead and she was the only one left out of the family besides her mother. She didn't consider her mother family anymore and probably never would again. A tear fell down her cheek and she quickly wiped it away. A sudden ping of guilt ran through her about her sister, but she quickly brushed it off. She had been through so much in life. She would deal with Jennifer's death like she had everything else in her life; one step at a time.

***

Michael pulled up at his and Brittany's home, but decided to wait in the car for a second before going inside. He was worried about what was waiting for him on the other side of the door. He knew Brittany was probably going out of her mind just as much as he was. He just wasn't sure how to even talk to Brittany about everything. He knew he had to be there for her and to support her, but it was deeper than that. He wanted to make sure that she knew he was just as scared and worried as she was. There was only one way to deal with everything and that was to go inside. He turned the car off and walked up the steps to their house. Not much changed over the years, just a few things here and there that he added, but overall nothing major. He loved the house the way it was and didn't want to change anything. He looked over at the rocking chairs that were now on the porch. He and Brittany had picked them up at the local flea market not long after they were married. Brittany didn't like them too much at the time because she said they made her feel like they were old people, but she let Michael win that debate.

Michael opened the door, took his shoes off, and locked the door back behind him. He waited for a second to see if he could hear Brittany moving around. At first, he didn't hear anything, but then he heard the slightest sound. It sounded like water running so he guessed she was upstairs running herself a bath. He went to the kitchen and laid his keys down on the island. He made the decision to give her a little while longer to relax and then he would go up and check on her. He sat down at the island and pulled out his phone. Checking it, he noticed his friend Mark had sent him a text earlier that day. He opened the text to see what was going on.

Hey bud! What r u and Britt doing this weekend? Wanna get together Sat and grill out at our place?

Michael sighed and wondered if it would be a good idea to even text Mark back. He didn't want to share the news about the baby yet because he hadn't even talked to Brittany. He decided to just leave it up in the air and keep the conversation on another topic instead.

Hey man! I have no clue what Britt has planned but I'll let you know. How r u and Taylor?

Cool. Taylor is good. Still doing her therapy, but getting better. We will talk more about this weekend later though. Hit me up later in the week man!

NP man. Talk to you then!

The water had stopped running so he guessed she was soaking and relaxing by then. Michael put his phone down and started walking up the stairs to his and Brittany's room. He opened the door to their room and headed straight to the bathroom. The curtain was closed around the claw foot tub so he decided to take his clothes off and get in with Brittany.

He laid his clothes in a neat pile next to the double sink and pulled back the curtain. Brittany had the water up to the rim with bubbles overflowing. She looked up at him and smiled. Slowly his worries started to melt away. Giving Brittany space was always the best thing to do.

Michael slid in the tub. As he heard the water flow over the sides, he was glad Brittany had a drain put in the floor when she built the house otherwise he would have had a mess on his hands. Michael felt Brittany's legs touch his and his heart beat started growing faster. No matter how many years they had been together Brittany would always make him feel like he never had before. He looked over at Brittany and noticed she was smiling at him.

"What did I do?"

She laughed softly and rolled her eyes at him.

"Nothing. It's just sometimes in the worst situations you can still make me smile and not even mean to."

His smile faded for a second as he thought, does this mean that she isn't happy about the baby? Should I ask her about it? He figured he would wait a little while longer before bringing it up. Then an idea came to his mind.

"Hey, can I take you somewhere once you're done relaxing?"

Brittany looked at him with a grin and said, "Of course, you can but where?"

"It's a surprise. Just take as long as you need and once you're done then get ready and meet me downstairs."

He stood up from the tub letting the water run down his body. He kissed her on the cheek and got out of the tub. After getting dressed, Michael went to the kitchen to get some stuff together before Brittany got done. He rushed to get everything he needed and took everything to the car. As he walked back to the house, he almost ran into Brittany in the hallway. He stopped suddenly, amazed by how beautiful she was. She was always beautiful to him, but there was something different about her that day. She had a glitter in her eyes, her hair seemed lighter, and her lips seemed plumper. Kissing her on the cheek, he took another long look at her.

"Are you ready to go?"

Brittany nodded and Michael grabbed her hand. He led her out the door to the car. He was excited to take her away from their normal life for a little while. He just hoped she liked where he was taking her. He would find out soon enough.

***

Brittany laughed when Michael pulled her to the car. He sure was excited about taking her wherever it was. Once they got into the car, Michael looked at her and smiled before handing her a cloth. She took it from him but didn't understand.

"What's this for?"

Smiling he looked over at her, and said "I'm going to blindfold you for the trip; I don't want you to know where we are going."

Brittany smiled and nodded. It wasn't like she could argue about it because he was so excited about wherever they were going it would kill him if she did. Michael placed the blindfold over her eyes and tied it in the back. Slowly he pulled out of the driveway. She tried to follow the road with her memory, but eventually she gave up because he took so many turns she had no clue where they really were. She could feel his hand holding hers and his finger gliding over her hand slowly. It helped ease her mind having him touching her.

Over time she wondered if they were leaving the state because it seemed like they were driving forever. Suddenly she could feel the car going over some bumps and knew they were getting close to their destination. Eventually the car came to the stop and she tried to listen for signs of where they were. The engine to the car was off, but there were no signs of cars around her so she guessed they were in the country. She heard Michael open his door, the car shift when he got out, and his door close. She almost jumped when her door opened because it was so quiet. She could hear him laugh under his breath.

"Can I take this thing off now?"

Michael didn't say anything and instead helped her out of the car. She took two steps and then he stopped her.

"What do you hear and smell?"

She took in a deep breath and waited for her senses to kick in. Not being able to see helped her other senses come out full blast. She felt the wind sweep in from behind her and her hair softly hit her face. Birds were singing all around her and she could even hear an owl not far away. She could feel the sun hitting her face and the cold bitter air sent goose bumps over her skin. She was lost in her own world and a vision she made up. She smelled Michael close behind her and started to smile.

Michael grabbed her hand and asked, "Do you know where you are Britt?"

She could only shake her head. She really had no clue where she was but she knew it was wonderful. Then her blindfold was undone and she was breathless at where they were. A tear ran down her cheek and she could feel herself coming undone inside. Before she knew it, tears were streaming down her face and even a sob came out of her mouth. She was filled with so much happiness and emotions that she couldn't take it. She turned and hugged Michael hoping she would hold this memory in her heart forever.

CHAPTER FIVE

Three days had passed since Tiffany had to identify her sister's body. She still couldn't shake the fact that her sister was really dead. She asked the detectives if they had any leads on who did it but still nothing. The only thing they told her was they were waiting for some prints to come back before they could possibly have a suspect.

It was the day she had to bury her sister. She made sure to put it in the local paper to let everyone know Jennifer had passed away. Not talking to Jennifer for over six years meant that she didn't know anyone that was involved in her life. She didn't know if she had a boyfriend, friends, or even coworkers. She had no clue about anything that involved Jennifer.

Jennifer was young, but very smart. She left a will and Tiffany guessed it was because she had a business and sometimes they require you to have a backup plan for when or if you die. The crazy part was Jennifer left it all to Tiffany and she couldn't figure out why. The even harder part was what the hell she was going to do with everything? Tiffany planned to ride over to Jennifer's house after the funeral to go through her stuff. She needed to figure out what to do with everything and then there were the issues of Jennifer's business. She thought about selling it, but she had a ping of guilt hit her. That was all Jennifer had and she didn't know if she could push herself to sell it. She would deal with everything one step at a time.

Tiffany finished getting dressed and decided to go to the funeral home early. She hoped some people would show up and give her a little bit of information about her sister's life. She meet Jennifer's friend Alexis at the funeral home.

Alexis was one of Jennifer's close friends. She told Tiffany that Jennifer didn't have a boyfriend and hadn't dated since she had known her. The chatted for a bit, but at the end of the day Tiffany didn't gain much more information about her sister then she had prior to the funeral.

Tiffany drove straight to Jennifer's apartment and hoped she would find something to let her know more about her sister. She did find out from Alexis that Jennifer had a cat named Missy. Tiffany hoped the thing was still alive after being home alone for a few days. Trying to figure out what to do with all her sisters stuff was one thing, but now there was a cat. She was not a fan of cats and probably never would be, but she would take it home and at least try to find a good home for it.

Driving through town, Tiffany saw her sister's boutique. She made a mental note to stop by the shop on the way back home. Her focus at that time was to see what was in her sister's house. She parked in the parking lot of the apartment and walked to her Jennifer's door. She dialed the number of the landlord and waited for them to finally answer.

"Hello," a lady said.

"Yes, my sister was Jennifer Childress and she recently passed. I need to get in her home to gather some things and wondered if you had a key?"

The lady sighed.

"Yes, I'll be right over. Give me just a moment."

Tiffany didn't have to wait long at all before the lady showed up.

"So, you're the sister that she never talked to?"

Feeling a little embarrassed Tiffany nodded.

"Well here is the key. The rent is paid up for the next two months so take your time getting the things out. If you get the stuff out before the rents up then I'll gladly give you the money back for it."

The lady was gone just as fast as she got there. All she could think about was how weird that was. Once Tiffany opened the door, the past slapped her in the face. Goose bumps went all over her body and her hands began to sweat. It was going to be much harder than she ever thought.

***

Brittany couldn't believe that Michael brought her back to the meadows after all those years. She loved that place so much and always wondered why they never came back to it. Then again, they were always busy with work or just normal day to day things. She needed to come there more than he could understand. After all the things they had been through many years ago, that place was where she and Michael could go to get away from the world. It was the best thing Michael could have done to get her away from everything. Michael was behind her waiting and watching to see what she would do or say. All she could do is smile and wipe away the tears.

Brittany walked over to the cliff; which was her favorite thing about the place. For miles and miles there was no sign of human life. It was just trees, wildlife, and a water fall. She took in a deep breath and let it out slowly. The smell and sounds of that place calmed her mind. She heard a door shut and turned to see what Michael was doing. He had a blanket in one hand and a basket in his other. With a big smile on his face, he walked to the middle of the meadow, set down the basket, and unfolded the blanket. Brittany couldn't help but feel like she was back in time to the first time they went there. Michael brought food, a blanket, a spy glass, flowers, a radio and an envelope. She sat down on the blanket and couldn't get over everything that he brought. She looked around trying to see what was missing and at first she couldn't remember what it was. Then it hit her. There was a camera the last time they came there. Michael noticed her look and picked up the envelope.

"I know you're wondering where the camera is, but I thought I would bring this instead."

When he handed her the envelope she looked up at him confused. Brittany opened the envelope and started crying all over again. Inside were the pictures from the first visit.

"These are from our first date, Britt. I never got the chance to show them to you so I put them up for a special time."

He took his hand and wiped the tears off her cheek. She flipped through the pictures and couldn't help but laugh at some of them. There were a few of Michael and a goofy face he was making at her. Then she saw some of the ones where she was standing at the cliff. She hadn't changed much over the years and neither had Michael. It was more of the fact that it brought her back to when she first fell in love with Michael. Their life was so hard back then, but they had come such a long way since then.

Brittany felt Michael's hand touch hers and it brought her back to the present.

"Britt, I wanna talk to you about the baby. Just hear me out, okay?"

Brittany had a feeling it was going to come up and she

was happy he brought it up and not her. She nodded and waited for him to gather his words.

"Britt, I know we didn't expect this at all and trust me it's a shock to me just as it is to you. I just want you to know that I'm not going anywhere. I am in this with you through whatever happens. I just want to know what you think about everything."

Brittany didn't know where to start. Of course, she was shocked by the baby but she didn't know what to do. At that point, there wasn't much she could do about it. She refused to abort the baby and she could never give the baby up. So, the decision was made that she was keeping the baby no matter what. She just couldn't get over the shock of it all.

"I don't want you to think I am upset about finding out about the baby because that's not it. I have always wanted kids but I never thought it would happen. So, when the doctor said that we were having a baby it was a total shock to me in more ways than one. I have already chosen to keep the baby and I hope that is okay with you, Michael. Like the doctor said, I am healthy for my age and I think we would make great parents. I am a little nervous about labor, but I think I will be okay. I mean what choice do I really have not to be. In the long run, we will have to figure out some minor things but for now we take this one step at a time, okay?"

Michael smiled at her, leaned over, and placed a kiss on her cheek. She couldn't be happier than she was at that moment. Her life was great and now she would have a baby to bring into this world.

"I love you, Britt and we will do every step together."

***

When Tiffany shut the door behind her, she didn't know if she could move. It felt weird to be standing in her sister's house. There was art work all around her on the walls. Once you went into the front door, the rest of the apartment was open. The living room and kitchen didn't have any walls separating them. The walls were painted a gray color, almost a pale blue. Her sister had great taste in decorating. Tiffany recognized some of the art work on the walls as Salvador Dali. He was always one of their favorite artists growing up. She was surprised to see some of his art work in Jennifer's house because his work wasn't cheap. Then again it could be just a knock off, but she wasn't sure. Either way, she would have to make sure to keep them put away. Jennifer would never forgive her if she sold or got rid of them.

In the living room, there was a flat screen TV hanging on the wall and a coffee table in the middle of the floor. Jennifer didn't own much furniture because there was only a couch in the living room, which was surprising because the living room was pretty big. Tiffany looked over at the kitchen and saw the counter tops were a dark black and there were a few dishes in the sink. The only thing on the counters was a knife block and a coffee maker. Tiffany remembered how much Jennifer loved coffee. Tiffany couldn't help but laugh at one of the memories. Tiffany never owned a coffee maker and when Jennifer moved in with her it was hell when Jennifer didn't have coffee in the morning.

Walking down a hall that was past the kitchen and living room, Tiffany found three closed doors. She decided to look in the first room to the right. Inside she found a laundry room that was way neater then hers would ever be. There were shelves everywhere and labels for everything. There wasn't a washer or dryer so she guessed that Jennifer must have used ones the apartment supplied. Tiffany closed the door and turned to the other two doors. She decided to open the one across from the laundry room. It was Jennifer's bathroom. The bathroom was bright and white with a dark green trim. There were dark green towels hanging up and the shower curtain and rugs matched. Tiffany couldn't get over how everything had a special place.

Jennifer's home was clean, neat, and organized. Tiffany could remember having to tell her sister to clean up after herself all the time, so it was definitely not something she had expected. She closed the door to the bathroom and went into the last door; Jennifer's bedroom. The walls were a bright pink with a dark black trim. That room felt more like the Jennifer that Tiffany remembered. The bed covers were black to match the trim. There was more art work on the walls in this room just like the others. Tiffany couldn't recognize who the artist was, but she liked all the paintings.

There was a noise coming from under the bed and at first Tiffany didn't know what it was then the thought hit her, the cat. Just as the thought crossed her mind a black and gray fluff ball came out from under the bed. It had to have been the biggest cat Tiffany had ever seen. The cat wasted no time before it came right up to her and started to rub on her legs.

"Oh Lord. I hate cats, so me and you aren't going to get along."

She sighed and looked around some more. When Tiffany scanned the room, she noticed an animal carrier under a desk in the corner. *That will come in handy,* she thought as she walked out of the room. She headed to the kitchen to find the cat some food. The cat kept in step with her and whined the whole time. Tiffany started to search all the cabinets and finally found it under the sink. She grabbed the bag and the cat bowls and headed back to the bedroom. After putting the cat into the carrier she tucked the food and bowls under her arms and decided to leave. She had enough of being in her sister's house for one day. Now that Jennifer was gone she had to get over the fact that she didn't even know her sister at all and that hurt.

CHAPTER SIX

Michael pulled into the driveway at his and Brittany's home. He was glad he made the choice to take Brittany to the meadow. They both needed to get away from life for a little while and that was the best place to do it. Michael jumped out of the car and ran around to open Brittany's door. She got out and gave him a frown.

"Don't start that crap with me Michael. I have heard stories where the guy starts doing everything for the woman when she is pregnant thinking the girl can't do it. I am not that type of girl and if you do that, I will throat punch you!"

All Michael could do was laugh and shake his head. Brittany didn't keep her serious face long before she coughed out a laugh. They both headed inside to enjoy what was left of their day.

After getting comfortable on the couch Michael started flipping through all the channels on the TV. However, he was not paying attention to anything that came on. His mind was on the baby and Brittany.

"So when do you want to start telling everyone?"

Brittany gave him a surprised look.

"Well you aren't supposed to tell anyone for a while, you know just in case."

Michael knew what that meant and he didn't like it. In fact that thought hadn't even crossed his mind yet. What if they did lose the baby? He knew he wouldn't be able to take it. Brittany must have seen his face.

"Michael, I'm sure everything is going to be fine. Look, I will call a local OBGYN tomorrow and get an appointment, okay? For now, we will just tell our closest friends. You can tell Mark and I'll tell Taylor. Deal?"

Michael knew she was right. He would just think good things until they saw the doctor. He was happy he could tell someone because he didn't know if he could keep it to himself.

"Well, I'm glad you brought up telling Mark and Taylor because Mark invited us over to eat this weekend."

"Well, we will both tell them then. No telling until then!"

Brittany gave him a stern look and he knew she meant business.

"You don't have to worry about me talking, Britt. I don't see Mark everyday like you do Taylor."

Brittany rolled her eyes and look at the TV. They finally found a movie on and curled up on the couch to watch it.

Early in the morning, Michael woke up alone on the couch with the sun shining into the house. Rubbing his eyes and yawning, he looked around for Brittany. He finally heard water running and guessed she was getting ready for work. He got up and walked to the kitchen to make some coffee. After putting on the coffee, he headed upstairs to take a shower with Brittany. When he walked into the bathroom he found Brittany face first at the toilet throwing up.

"Britt, are you okay?"

Brittany tried to say yes between breaths. Michael was worried. Was that normal for pregnant women to do? Was the baby okay? Michael grabbed a rag and ran it under warm water. He dropped to his knees on the floor beside Brittany and rubbed her back until she finished. Brittany slumped to the side and leaned against the wall.

"I'm fine, Michael, and this is normal. Some women have morning sickness for months while they're pregnant."

Still worried he handed her the rag. He didn't know how she could do that for months and he wished he could take the sickness from her.

"Do you need anything?"

Brittany shook her head and started to stand up. Michael helped her to her feet and made sure she could balance herself before letting go. Slowly Brittany took her clothes off and got into the shower with him right behind her. They took turns washing each other and eventually got out.

A little while later, Brittany left for work and Michael got some files out of the cold case box. At first he didn't know if his mind would let him work, but eventually it started on the right track. Around lunch time Michael needed a break from papers. Up until that point nothing in the box came up as anything that could be closed easily. Most of the cases were only a few years old and seemed to hit a dead end. There was only one in the box that he felt had a chance at being solved and after lunch he was going to look into it. It was so far a pretty solid case. A woman was murdered twelve years prior and there were no leads to who did it. There was some DNA left at the scene, but it didn't match anyone in the database. He planned on trying to run the DNA again and see if he got any hits. It looked like the last time it was run was seven years prior so maybe the scum bag messed up and got into some trouble since then. But first a tuna sandwich was calling his name.

***

Tiffany didn't stay long at Jennifer's shop because she had the cat in the car. Cats in cold weather didn't do too well. She would just have to make a trip back by there in the next few days. Plus she had to stop at the store and get some stuff for the cat.

She didn't realize she would be walking out with a buggy full of stuff. The more she thought about it the more she realized the cat was probably going to stay with her. She bought things like a litter box, litter, cat tower, toys, food, cat bed, and cat nip. *This better be a good cat,* she thought hoping she didn't regret buying all the stuff.

Tiffany walked in the door with everything; she managed to get it all in one trip. Putting the cat carrier down, she opened it and the cat flew out. She figured it was scared and run off but hoped in a few days it would come around. She set the cat tower up in the living room and put the bed beside it with the toys in it. Then she put the bowls in the kitchen and made sure to fill them up with food and water. She called out to the cat, but it never came. She figured it would eventually be hungry and come out. Now that she got the cat settled she could finally relax.

The words hit her mind and she immediately wished them back because there was a knock at the door. She had no idea who was at her house and why. She was beyond tired and didn't want to deal with anyone so it better had been good. She walked to her door and looked out the peephole. There stood the two detectives from the other day. She opened the door and let them in.

"What can I do for y'all this evening?"

Watson stood back and watched his partner do all the talking.

"We are here to place you under arrest, Ms. Childress. We found your prints on the murder weapon at your sister's crime scene. It seems a little strange they would be there since you stated that you haven't talked to or seen your sister in over six years."

Tiffany couldn't believe what she was hearing. Was she really being arrested for murdering her sister? Were they stupid or what? Why the hell would she want to kill her? *There's no way this is real.* Sure enough, Watson walked over to where she was and pulled her arms behind her back and placed cuffs on her.

"You have got to be kidding me! I didn't kill my sister! You have this all wrong because I haven't seen her in six years! Plus why in the hell would I kill her?"

They never answered her. All she could hear was Watson reading her rights to her. Tears filled her eyes and she suddenly felt more anger towards her sister right then. None of this made sense at all but she would get a lawyer to prove it was a lie.

***

Michael pulled up at the office and got out. The wind was howling like crazy and if people weren't careful they would get frost bite. He opened the doors to the building and the warm air slapped him in the face. He knew he had to slip past his chief because being gone only one day wouldn't be enough for him. Michael didn't have plans for staying at work though. He just wanted to run the DNA and get back home. Well that's what his mind was telling him up until he walked into work. All of a sudden he didn't want to go back home. He didn't know what to do when he wasn't working. The only thing that could come to mind was yard work and it was way too cold for that.

Michael made it to his desk without anyone major seeing

him. He sat down and wrote out the email to the lab to run the DNA again. He really hoped they would get a hit in the database because if not then he had no work. It would be a few days before the lab would get back to him so in the meantime he planned on looking into the new case that Watson and Matthews were working. There was no way he was sitting around an office doing nothing all day or at home. Just as he pushed send on the email to the lab he looked up and saw his chief staring at him.

"I know I'm supposed to be home working on cold cases, but I had to run some old DNA on a murder years ago."

Chief Belue raised an eyebrow then said, "I'm not here to get onto you about being here. I was actually going to call you, but the girl up front said you had rushed by."

Michael got the feeling his boss had a job for him and wanted him back just as bad as he wanted to be back.

"Okay, so what did you need Boss?"

He waved for Michael to follow him as he slowly walked away.

"Do you remember the case about the girl found in the dumpster that Matthews and Watson were working on?"

Michael nodded and made sure his chief saw him.

"Well, we found prints on the weapon and DNA on the body. Here is the thing. Just as we were about to close it and take it to court the suspect said she wanted to see you."

Michael stopped dead in his tracks. *Who the hell would want to talk to me?*

"I know it's weird, Michael, and I don't think you know her. Just the way she acts tells us that she doesn't know you. She claims she is innocent and didn't do it, but it's a pretty solid case. Look, you don't even have to talk to her. I only told her I would let you know, so I did."

Michael started to walk when his chief did. He was still confused but knew it would eat him alive if he didn't see who the girl was and what she wanted.

"I'll go see what she wants. If I don't it will bother me. Besides, I'm waiting on DNA anyway."

Chief Belue nodded and headed down the hall to his office and Michael turned down the hall towards the interrogation rooms.

After sending an officer to pull the girl from lock up, Michael sat down in one of the rooms. A few minutes later the door opened and a girl walked in with the officer right behind her. He locked her cuffs to the table and left them alone. The girl wasn't anyone he had ever seen before and Michael was confused at what she wanted with him. She had brown, curly hair that came down to her shoulders and tons of freckles all over her face. She had a childish look about her, but her eyes gave away her age. She looked away from him like she was embarrassed that he was looking at her.

"I was told that you asked for me and I have to say I'm confused as to why."

The girl looked him in the eye before speaking. He had no idea she was about to take him back in time.

***

Brittany was having a slow day at work. Taylor on the other hand was busy bothering her all day. Brittany knew that if Taylor came in her office one more time and bugged her about why she didn't come back to work the day before she would be forced to tell Taylor. Just as she was thinking that, Taylor walked in her office. Brittany sighed and rolled her eyes at Taylor.

"Taylor, sit down. We need to talk about something."

Suddenly Taylor's face changed to a worried look.

"Okay. What's going on Britt?"

Brittany almost didn't want to tell her because she promised Michael they would tell her and Mark both that weekend.

"Look, I'm not supposed to tell you this so promise you won't say anything. I promised Michael I would wait until this weekend to tell you."

Taylor nodded and Brittany stood up and walked over to where Taylor was.

"I went to the doctor yesterday and I found out Michael and I are going to have a baby."

Before Brittany could say another word, Taylor was jumping up and down. She hugged Brittany and said, "I knew it! I so knew it!"

Brittany hugged her back. When Taylor was finally done squeezing her she stood back to finish what she was saying.

"Michael and I were going to tell you and Mark this weekend so when we do you better act shocked just like you did. We are shocked ourselves and taking it one step at a time."

Taylor started crying and then sat down on the couch.

"Britt, this is so great. Congratulations!"

Brittany got the feeling there was another reason Taylor was crying. Brittany sat down next to Taylor and looked her in the eyes.

"What's wrong? And don't forget I know you all too

well."

Taylor smiled and grabbed Brittany's hand.

"Mark and I asked y'all to come over this weekend because we wanted to tell y'all that we are having a baby."

Brittany was the one jumping up and down now.

"This is so amazing Taylor! I was so scared I was going to go through this alone but now we can do this together!"

Brittany sat down and hugged Taylor tight. Taylor laughed really loud and tears started to fall down Brittany's cheek.

"How far along are you Britt?"

"I'm around five weeks but we have to go see an OBGYN to confirm it. What about you?" Taylor smiled big. "I'm around seven weeks! We are searching for a good doctor to go see too! We should see the same doctor. This is so great Britt; I am so excited for us both."

Brittany suddenly felt her worries about the baby fly away. She had her best friend to go through the process with her and it would take some of the worries off her. Now she had to act just as surprised as Taylor would have to be. It was going to be hard to do but as happy as she was feeling she knew she could do it.

***

Tiffany looked into Michael's eyes and prayed he would help her. She had to lay it all out on the table for him and just keep praying.

"I'm going to start at the beginning so bear with me on this, okay. I'll make it as short as I can but we both know no story is short, that's why it's called a story. My dad died when I was young and not long after he died my mother left. I had a sister named Jennifer who became my life. After getting out of foster homes, I got my own place and went to school while working two, sometimes three, jobs. I took Jennifer in and helped her build a life because she was the only family I ever had. Eventually she had an affair with someone I was going to marry. I left her and him without looking back. For six years, I had no contact with my sister. I hurt for many years not only because she slept with him but because I lost the only family I ever had. Then one day I had two cops show up and say she was found dead. That crushed me for more reasons than one and I was forced to go ID her body. I forced myself to bury my sister and collect her things. Do you have any idea how hard that is, especially when I had no idea who my sister even was six years later? I could eventually deal with all of that but when they put me in cuffs and told me I killed my sister, that was something I could never deal with. I am being framed just like you were. I know about how you were framed for a murder that you didn't do and I'm not asking for a lot. I am only asking for you to look closer and see that I didn't kill my own sister! There has to be some evidence showing that I never did this. Michael, help me please. I am begging you."

She could feel herself shaking from being so upset. Tears were rolling down her face and she had no intentions on stopping them. Michael was her only chance at fixing her mess and they both knew it. Now it was up to him to make a decision.

***

Everyone always screamed that they are innocent and Tiffany was no different. Or was she? Michael had no idea why, but something inside him told him that she didn't kill her sister. Then again when he was framed there wasn't much evidence against him. With her case, there was DNA evidence and finger prints. So, either this was just her wanting to manipulate him or she really was innocent. He didn't have anything else to do right then until his DNA came back on the cold case. His gut was telling him that she didn't do it, so he figured it wouldn't hurt to look into it.

"I'll do what I can but you have to be honest with me all the way. I'll talk to my chief and see if he will allow me some time to look into things. Now, do you have any idea who would want to frame you? Who would want your sister dead? Anyone who hates your sister or you? It's important that you think back long and hard because killers can go back years and wait for the right time to strike."

She looked down at the table.

"The only people that hated me in my life was my ex and my sister. I don't know enough about my sister's new life to tell you if anyone hated her or not. As far as I know there wasn't anyone that didn't love my sister. My dad is dead and my mother ran off. She didn't have any reason to hate us but then again why would she leave us alone."

"Are you sure your father was dead? Also, do you know where you mother is?"

Michael hated asking her that but he had no choice after what he went through.

"Yes, I am sure my father is dead. He died in a car wreck and I was there to see him buried."

Michael had a feeling the case was going to be a lot more trouble than he had imagined.

"What were your mother's and father's names? I will also need your ex's name."

Tiffany nodded at him and he slid her a paper and pen to write all the names down. She handed him the paper and he stood up to leave. Before he opened the door, he heard her start to say something.

"Thank you, Michael. Even if this ends up getting pinned on me, thank you for trying."

He flashed a half smile before he turned to leave.

CHAPTER SEVEN

Brittany couldn't believe that her best friend was going to have a baby really close to the same time she was. She could only imagine how Michael would feel once he knew about the news. It was around four o'clock when Brittany closed her lap top and walked to Taylor's desk. Taylor was typing away on the computer when Brittany walked up to her.

"I'm heading out. Why don't you do the same? It's been a slow day today, so it won't hurt if we leave a little early."

Taylor looked up from her computer and smiled.

"Okay, great. Hey, you want to go grab some food? We don't have to tell the guys and let's face it we will be hungry again by dinner time tonight. After all we do have a pretty good excuse to eat a lot."

Brittany could only laugh. She was up for getting something to eat because they both skipped lunch.

"Okay so what do you want to eat? Don't say tacos either, because I want to throw up just at the thought of that."

Taylor laughed and closed her computer.

"Okay, so let's just get some subs and talk, okay?"

Brittany nodded and they both headed to the front door.

Once at the local sub shop, Brittany placed her order for a cold cut sub; nothing fancy because her stomach still wasn't doing well with all foods. Taylor got the same thing and they both sat down at a booth.

Taylor was the first to speak, "So, we might have a new case but it's hard to explain."

Brittany took a sip of her drink and looked at Taylor questionably.

"Well, you remember the girl that they found across town stabbed to death in the dumpster? Well they found her sister's DNA and fingerprints on the weapon and her body. Here is the kicker though; she claims to not have talked to her sister in over six years. Apparently, they had a fall out over a guy and she left. Now six years later her sister is dead and she gets pinned for it. She claims she didn't do it. The word on the streets is that she demanded to talk to Michael about it today. It sounds pretty easy to close but she says she was framed and thinks Michael could help her."

Brittany was shocked she hadn't heard anything about the case yet. Plus, Michael wasn't supposed to be at work for a few days because he was working on cold cases.

"Why didn't you tell me, Taylor?"

Taylor shrugged her shoulders and looked up at the server bringing them their food. They both said thank you and took the food.

"Well, I didn't tell you because it hasn't been confirmed that we have the case yet. I'm still waiting on the office to fax over the rest of the reports to me and let me know if we have it or not."

Brittany took a bite of her sandwich and was surprised that her stomach seemed grateful for the food. She expected to throw it right back up.

"Well, let me know first thing if we get it."

Taylor only nodded because she was devouring her sandwich just like Brittany was. Brittany put the case in the back of her mind for the time being, because food was the only thing she wanted to think about. She could always talk to Michael later about the case.

***

Brittany pulled into her driveway feeling like she weighed a hundred pounds heavier. She ended up eating a full sub, half of another and a slice of chocolate pie. She had never eaten so much in her life and there was defiantly no way she would be able to eat dinner with Michael later that night.

She got out of the car and made sure she locked it back after she grabbed her purse. At first, she didn't even realize that Michael's truck wasn't in the driveway. Brittany looked down at her phone and saw the time; it was five thirty. That was weird. Michael was always home by then even if he had to work over he always let her know. Brittany went into the house and sat her stuff down on the island. She picked up her phone and tried to call Michael. It ended up going straight to his voicemail. Brittany felt a little worried, but she soon brushed it off. Maybe his phone just died and he wasn't able to call her to let her know he would be late. She decided to run upstairs and shower before he got home.

***

Michael got into his truck and started the drive home. It was five-fifteen before he left the station. He got Chief Belue to give him two weeks before taking further action against Tiffany. Michael looked over at the files in his seat and then looked back at the road. He forgot to call Brittany and let her know he would be a little late getting home. He just hoped he hadn't worried her much at all.

Michael turned on his road and went around the first curve. He wasn't driving fast, but he slowed down anyway because for some reason an eerie feeling crept up on him. A feeling that was warranted, because out of nowhere there was a person standing on the side of the road with a jacket and a mask pulled up over their face. He knew it was cold out but did they really need the mask? Suddenly the person turned, faced Michael's truck, and pulled out a gun.

Michael was glad he saw the person when he did because it gave him just enough time to jerk the wheel. He heard the shot go off but it was too late for him. Michael jerked the wheel too hard and he went off the road. The ditch caught his truck and sent it flying in the air; flipping out of control. During that time all Michael could think about was Brittany and the baby. His truck hit the ground hard and rolled two more times before a tree stopped it. Michael was knocked out when the truck slammed into the ground. The last image that played into his mind was Brittany.

***

Brittany got out of the shower, got dressed and ran downstairs. She checked her phone again to see if Michael had called or texted. Still nothing and now it was five-fifty. She tried really hard to not let her mind get the best of her, but her gut was screaming something was wrong. She decided to call into the station and see if he had left yet. She hoped that was where he was and his phone died and he was still stuck at work. The phone rang two times before a woman answered the phone.

"Rocky Creek Falls Sheriff's Office. How can I help you?"

Brittany took a deep breath and finally let the words come to her.

"Yes, this is Brittany Sims. I'm calling to speak to my

husband Michael Sims. Can you patch me through to his desk please?"

"Hold on one second please."

The phone made a beeping noise and she waited for Michael to pick up. The only problem was that it wasn't Michael that answered the phone. Brittany could feel her heart pick up speed and her hands start to shake.

"Brittany...This is Grayson Belue...I was on my way to call you when my secretary paged me and said you were on the line...I don't know how to say this, but Sims was in an accident a few minutes ago. We have people out in the field getting him to safety now."

Tears were running down Brittany's face, and her hands were shaking so hard she was surprised she was still holding the phone. Finally, she took a breath and spoke.

"What kind of accident? Is he okay?" She could tell she was talking fast and was shocked she even got the words out of her mouth.

"He got into a wreck off of Saddle Way Road and I'm not going to lie to you, it's bad. He is trapped in the truck and they are working to get him out. Brittany?"

When Brittany heard him say the road name she knew Michael was on their road and he was coming home when he wrecked. She hung up the phone, shoved it in her purse, and grabbed the keys. Getting to Michael was the only thing on her mind.

Brittany pulled out of their driveway flinging gravel as she did. She slowed her car a little because it wasn't just her she had to worry about and Michael wouldn't be happy if she wrecked going to help him. All she could picture was Michael's face. Was he okay? *He has to be okay. He promised that he would be there for me step by step with the baby.* Brittany felt the tears fall down her face again but she didn't care. When she rounded the first curve on their road she saw fire trucks blocking the road. There was a line of cars waiting to go around but Brittany wasn't waiting. She pulled around the cars and parked off the road. She jumped out of the car. One of the fire fighters came over telling her to get back in her car. She never even looked over at him and didn't think about the words coming out of her mouth.

"Try to stop me and I'll put your ass on the ground. That's my husband and I'm going to help him."

The fire fighter didn't move another step and Brittany started to run to where the commotion was. Off in the distance she could see smoke coming near a tree and heard yelling. When she saw Michael's truck she stopped dead in her tracks. It was against a tree and smashed in on all sides. The field was torn up where his truck flipped and slid across the ground. Brittany forced her feet to move and she ran across the field to where fire fighters were working to get Michael out. There were three men working to put out the fire where the engine was. Then there were four men throwing a blanket over the side of the truck and working with a machine to get the door off. Brittany knew they were using the jaws of life to get him out, so she stood back and gave them room to work. She didn't hear Michael saying anything and it made her heart beat faster. There were medics standing by with a bed and their bags in hand. All she could do right then was pray that Michael was okay.

The men got the fire put out and moved back to let the other men work on the door. One of the medics looked over at her, put a neck brace down, and walked to where she was standing.

"You must be a family member or friend. I wanted to give you a little comfort because you look a little pale. I did try to get him to respond to me, but he never did. I was able to tell he had a pulse and was breathing okay. He is alive, ma'am, and that should give you some comfort. We won't know more until we can get him out, but I want you to take deep breaths, okay? If you think it's too much, don't be too prideful to turn away."

Brittany was thankful to hear that he was alive. Her heart seemed to slow down a tiny bit, but not much. He was still stuck inside the truck and there was sure to be more injuries then they could tell right away. Just as she looked back up at the truck the firefighters were moving away and taking the door with them as they did. Just as the men moved out of her way of sight, the medics moved back into her way. She walked to where they were working because she just needed to see him. She needed to make sure he was in fact okay. She looked over the medic's shoulders and at that moment she wished she hadn't. Michael was bloody from head to toe. There was glass stuck all in his arms and in his face.

One of the medics pushed her back and yelled out towards the road, "We need some tools down here! Make it quick!"

Brittany looked the medic in the eyes and waited for them to explain what was going on. The medic must have noticed the look on her face because they finally spoke.

"He has metal from the truck imbedded into him. We can't risk taking it out of him because of bleeding so we need to cut the metal and let the hospital take it out with the right tools."

Brittany's heart stopped and she could feel the world around her spinning. All she could think was that Michael was going to die. What if it was hitting a major organ or even an artery? Soon her world went black and Brittany passed out on the ground.

CHAPTER EIGHT

Brittany woke up to a beeping noise and a headache. She tried to open her eyes, but they didn't want to. She fought to open them and once she did she wished she hadn't because the lights around her were way too bright. Brittany took a second to focus and to see where she was at. She looked around and saw machines going and a wrist band on her arm. Then it hit her that she was in a hospital and everything came flowing back to her.

"Michael!"

She sat up and threw off the covers, desperate to get to him. She suddenly felt someone grab her arm and she jumped. It was her dad.

"Brittany, calm down and take it easy, okay? You passed out and hit your head."

Brittany reached up and felt her head and sure enough there was a bump sticking up on the right side. She winced when she rubbed it and quickly put her hand back down.

"Where is Michael at, Dad?"

"He is in surgery right now, Brittany. He had some minor cuts and scrapes on his arms, legs, face, and back. The major wounds were in his stomach. A part of the truck door flew off and landed in his stomach. That's what he's in surgery for. The doctors are hopeful because of how much fight he put up. He demanded to see you and when the medics told him you had passed out and were being taken to the hospital he went even more crazy. That man really loves you, Brittany."

Brittany flashed a smile for the first time since she first got home earlier that day. She had no clue what time it was but she didn't care. Her number one priority right then was talking to a doctor and finding out how Michael's surgery was going.

***

After Brittany got dressed, she went to the second floor of the hospital where Michael's surgery was taking place. She walked up to the front desk and waited for the nurse to stop running around to talk to her. Brittany's mind was all over the place and she just wanted Michael to be okay...She needed him to be okay.

"I am here about my husband. He's in surgery right now and I would like to talk to a doctor about what's going on."

The lady sat down at the desk and started typing.

"What's your husband's name ma'am?"

Brittany started to shake again just at the thought of saying his name. She was a breakdown waiting to happen.

"Michael Sims is his name. He had a car accident and was brought in. He is a detective as well."

The woman looked away from her and back at the computer. After typing for what seemed like hours the lady finally looked up at Brittany.

"He should be out soon, but I will go ahead and request a doctor to come in and explain the process of what is going on. The waiting room is right over there. Just go have a seat and try to relax, okay?"

Brittany wanted to yell at the lady because she wanted answers right then and not later, but she knew she wouldn't get anywhere by yelling.

Brittany took a seat by her dad and folded her hands in her lap. She started to shake her leg and stare into space. Her mind was on one thing and that was Michael. How did he wreck on a road that he had traveled on for many years now? Was there an animal that crossed the road and he swerved to miss it? Just as her mind started to ramble on about what happened to Michael a doctor appeared in the waiting room. Brittany jumped to her feet and her dad wasn't far behind her.

"Mrs. Sims here for Michael Sims?"

Brittany could only nod her head at that point.

"Well he is coming out of surgery now and doing okay. I'm not going to lie to you. It was a long and hard surgery. For a while it was touch and go. He lost a lot of blood once we removed the metal from his side. We managed to get it out and stop the bleeding, but let me say your husband is very lucky. Two more inches to the left and it would have hit an organ, which would have killed him. We have him stitched up and waiting to be moved to ICU. We also got all his other minor cuts stitched up and the glass removed from his body. He should only be in ICU for a day and then in a normal room for another day. I am willing to let him go the day after tomorrow, but he will be on very light duty for a few days."

Brittany nodded and tried to take in everything that the doctor was saying.

"Your husband is going to be fine, Mrs. Sims," the doctor said before he walked away.

Brittany slowly sat back down in the chair, put her hands over her face, and began to cry. She was more than grateful that Michael was okay, but it was the fact that she could have lost him at the snap of someone's fingers. Her dad pulled her close to him and held her while she cried.

**

Michael woke up in excruciating pain. He had no idea what happened to him, but he knew whatever it was it couldn't be good. Michael's mouth and throat were so dry that he almost choked on what saliva he did have in his mouth. He looked around the room and tried to sit up. He winced at the pain in his head and side. Pulling back the covers, he saw that his side was wrapped in bandages and was bleeding through them. He kept trying to remember what happened, but no matter how hard he tried nothing came to mind. His eyes locked on Brittany sleeping in the chair beside his bed. He soon realized he was in the hospital. Brittany looked tired and he didn't want to wake her up. He looked around for a button to push for a nurse. He finally found a red button on a long wire. He pushed it and waited.

A short older woman came walking through the door. Her eyes widen when she saw him sitting up.

"Mr. Sims, you're awake. How do you feel? Do you need anything?"

Michael nodded his head and waited for his voice to finally come to him.

"Something to drink and I am in some serious pain. What happened to me?"

The woman came over and checked his IV bag then pulled a computer over to where he was at.

"You should be able to have something to drink, but I'll check with the doctor first. I will get you some medicine for the pain as well. I can't tell you what happened, but I will get the doctor in here to talk to you okay?"

Michael leaned back and looked over at Brittany who was still sleeping.

"She has been by your side for a while now. She has insisted on not leaving until you woke up. I'll be right back with some water and some medicine." With that she pushed the computer back and walked out of the room.

Michael thought back to his day and all he could remember was being at work. He talked to Tiffany and managed to get Chief Belue to let him look over the case before prosecuting her. Then he got into his truck and drove home. He couldn't remember if he made it home because everything went black. Michael's head began to throb and he started to get dizzy. He stopped trying to think of what happened because it seemed to make things worse. He would wait on the doctor and admire his wife sleeping. Just as he was trying to relax a sharp pain stung him in his side and he couldn't help but let out a cry.

Brittany jumped up and Michael immediately felt bad for it. Brittany grabbed his hand and tears began to fall down her face. Michael wiped them away and kissed the top of her hand. Whatever happened to him must have been bad for Brittany to cry.

"You're awake. Let me go grab the nurse and let them know."

Michael pulled her hand back and looked at her with a smile. "I already talked to the nurse and she should be back soon with meds and a doctor."

Brittany sighed and sat back down in the chair. She was holding his hand so tight he was worried she was hurting herself.

"Britt, what happened to me?"

Brittany looked down at the floor and started to cry even

more. He waited for her to gather herself. She sighed and then spoke very softly.

"Michael, you had a wreck on our road. They don't know what caused it yet, but they did say that you went off the road. After you went off the road it caused you to flip the truck. A tree stopped your truck from flipping. You had a lot of minor cuts and scrapes, but the worst part was a piece of metal went into your side. You had to go through surgery to get it taken out but they managed to get it out safely. Do you remember anything about it?"

Michael could feel his head start to spin just thinking about it.

"No. The only thing that I remember was leaving work to come home. Then after that it's all a blur."

Just then the nurse walked in the room with a man following her. He was tall and young, maybe in his early thirties.

"Michael, it's great to see you're awake. I'm Doctor Jefferson. Linda tells me you're in some pain and thirsty?"

Michael nodded and watched the doctor walk over to the computer.

"Okay, well we are going to give you some pain medicine and some water. Sip the water slow and try not to sit up too much. Linda said that you are experiencing some memory loss. Is that true?"

Michael watched the nurse set a cup of water down on the table next to him. Then she drew up, what Michael guessed was pain medicine, and then pushed it through his IV. It didn't take long for Michael to feel it. First was the burn in his arm and then a quick numbness to his mind. He felt a warmth wash over him and his mind started to relax from all his thoughts. He felt the pain in his side slowly start to vanish and even began to feel tired. Michael knew it wouldn't be long and his mind would give out and he would fall fast asleep. Michael made sure to talk to the doctor before that happened.

"Yes that is true. Brittany told me what happened to me, but I need to know when I'm getting out of here. I have to figure out what caused me to wreck. I know that I didn't just run off the road, so there has to be a reason for it."

Doctor Jefferson pushed the computer away from him and walked to Michael.

"You should be able to go home tomorrow. Michael, even though I am letting you go home tomorrow you will still be on light duty for a while. You had major surgery done and you have to be careful to not open the stitches up. You have to keep the wounds clean and make sure you change your bandages on time. Speaking of that, your nurse is going to change your bandage. We will take this one off and clean the wound. We will leave it off your wound for a little bit so it can get some air. Then your nurse will be back to wrap you back up. After the nurse gets done, make sure you both get some rest. Brittany, make sure you're taking your medicine and have your head looked at one more time, okay?"

Michael looked over at Brittany. He was confused. He didn't understand why her head would need to be looked at.

"What happened to your head? Are you okay? What about the baby?"

Michael could see Brittany's face turn white. The doctor was almost out of the room when he heard Michael's questions.

"Michael, the baby is fine, and Brittany passed out at your wreck. She did get a minor concussion but she is okay. We gave her some medicine for the headaches and some prenatal vitamins also."

Michael watched the doctor walk out the door and watched the nurse come to his bedside.

"Can you lift the covers up and also your gown?"

Michael did as she asked and pulled up his sheets with his gown. He felt the bed start to move down and his side started to burn. The nurse must have seen the pain on his face because she stopped moving the bed.

"I'm going to get this bandage off and look at the wound, okay?"

Michael nodded and watched her pull back the start of the bandage. The nurse put one hand on Michael's shoulder and nudged him to lift his back up. He figured out why quickly. The nurse needed enough room to get the bandage out from behind his back where it was wrapped around him.

After a few times around, the nurse got the bandage undone. He could hear Brittany suck in a breath and he knew it must have been bad. Sure enough, when Michael looked down he saw just how bad the cut was. There was a line of stitches across his side that made the cut about five inches long. Michael was surprised at how clean the wound looked. There were a few spots that were bleeding but overall it seemed to be a really good job stitching. The nurse went to where the sink was and picked up a clear bottle and a few rags.

"This is some sterile cleaner for your wound. I can't lie to you, it will sting, but it will clean it."

Michael nodded and waited for the burning to start. Just as the nurse applied the rag to his wound there was a knock on the door. Brittany got up and went to see who it was. Michael didn't care who it was at that moment. He just wanted the burning to stop. When the nurse got done cleaning the wound, she pulled his gown back down.

"I'll be back in a bit to wrap it back up. I think you have company anyway."

Michael smiled at her as best as he could. The nurse walked out, and Brittany came back in, but she wasn't alone. Michael looked past Brittany and saw some familiar faces. Briggs was following Brittany into the room. Behind Briggs was his chief with what looked like a bag of food.

"Hey guys, it's good to see y'all."

Briggs smiled and came to Michael's bedside while his chief stood at the end of the bed. He tossed Michael the bag. Michael could smell that it was a burger. He didn't know just how hungry he was until he smelt the food.

"Thanks for the food, Boss."

He nodded and looked down at the floor.

"Michael, we are here to follow up on the accident. We know it's a little soon and Brittany said that your memory was a little fuzzy. Has anything come back to you yet?"

Michael shook his head.

"I remember talking to you and then leaving. I was driving home and that's where it goes black."

Michael's chief nodded his head and then put his hands into his pocket.

"Here's the thing Sims. We had your truck towed back to the lab and found some weird stuff. At first, we thought it was just an accident but then after some further investigation we concluded that it wasn't. I don't want to confuse you with all the details Sims, so I will just get to the point. There are three bullet holes in your truck that proves that someone shot at you."

Michael sat up and forgot about the pain. The mention of the bullet holes triggered his memory to come back.

"Michael, what is it?" Brittany asked.

Michael heard Brittany speaking, but only one thought came to his mind. Michael looked up at his chief and said, "There was a girl there."

CHAPTER NINE

It had been a week since the accident. Brittany worked from home to help take care of him and he was grateful, but the walls were quickly closing in on him. He was able to walk without grunting and he just wanted to get back to work. He did manage to have Briggs fill him in on what was going on, but it wasn't the same. He needed to be at work and digging into his case with the woman trying to kill him and also on Tiffany's case. Tiffany's case was tough. She had no alibi and no clue about who would want to frame her. Her mom was nowhere to be found. Michael felt like there was something up with that, but could not find a motive for her to frame Tiffany. He was stuck on the case and he couldn't get into work to figure anything out.

Michael sat down on the couch and looked down at his phone to check the time. Mark and Taylor were coming over to cook out since they missed their originally planned get together. After the accident Brittany insisted they have the cook out at their house. Michael was glad to have some interaction with other people. He felt trapped inside the house and if he didn't get air soon he was going to go stir crazy. Just as he was about to get up and go find Brittany, the doorbell rang.

"I got it, babe!"

Michael walked slowly to the front door and opened it. Taylor jumped up and hugged him around the neck. Michael hugged her back. When she squeezed him, he thought he was going to run out of air.

"Don't ever scare us like that again, okay?"

Mark tapped Taylor on the shoulder, and said "Hun, if you keep squeezing him like that he might not be alive in a minute."

Taylor laughed and let go of Michael's neck. Michael moved to the side and let them in the hallway.

"Brittany is just getting out of the shower so she will be down soon."

Taylor started walking by Michael and once she got past him she stopped in her tracks.

"I am going to run up and talk to her for a second. Can y'all take the cake I baked into the kitchen and then get the steaks out of the fridge? Oh, and can you start up the grill?"

Michael didn't even get a chance to answer before Taylor took off up the stairs. Mark laughed and patted Michael on the back.

They walked into the kitchen and talked about Mark's new position at his job. Michael finally started to relax a little bit and was excited to tell Mark and Taylor the news soon.

***

Brittany heard a knock at her bedroom door and knew it was Taylor. She heard the doorbell down stairs and figured they were there. She was finishing with her makeup when she heard the knock. She walked to the door and opened it.

"Britt, I am so excited to tell everyone! What about you?"

Brittany was excited but at the same time she was

worried about Michael. Monday he would be going back to work and she was scared. They had already been through so much over the years and now someone else was trying to kill him. It was like their nightmare was being relived.

"I'm excited, too! Don't forget to make it believable."

Taylor nodded and sat down on the bed. Brittany put on her last bit of eye liner.

"So, let's go do this."

Taylor jumped up and followed Brittany out of her room. Brittany could feel her heart racing and was worried that Michael would be able to tell she was hiding something. For a week she was able to hide the fact that she knew about Mark and Taylor's secret from him, so she figured she would be able to last a little while longer.

Brittany got downstairs and didn't see Mark or Michael anywhere around. Then she saw shadows reflect off the deck of the back porch.

"I told the guys to get the grill started so they should be outside."

Brittany nodded at Taylor who had passed her in the kitchen. Once outside, Brittany went to where Michael was standing. She made sure to hug him tight. She felt great to be standing beside him. He wrapped his arm around her waist and pulled her close to him. She couldn't imagine being anywhere else than there, at that moment. Taylor and Mark came over and stood near them. It was crazy how much they all had in common.

Brittany still went back to the day that she almost lost her best friend. Michael's dad didn't care who he killed in the end as long as Michael was dead and blamed for it. Brittany knew Michael still felt a lot of guilt for Mark and Taylor getting hurt. She could see it in his eyes every time he looked at Taylor or Mark. Michael was the one that surprised her most over the years. Once Michael killed his father and the truth finally came out that he didn't kill Ashley, everything changed. Brittany's dad started to accept that Michael was innocent and that he had made a mistake. What shocked her most was when Michael came to Brittany and told her he wanted to be a cop. She would never forget that day.

She was cooking dinner for them just a few weeks after Michael's name had been cleared of the charges. He came in from working and kissed her on the head. He sat on the table and asked Brittany to come talk to him. She knew he was deep in thought when he asked to talk to her. She joined him at the table and waited on him to finally talk. Michael ended up telling her he wanted to give justice to people that were in the same situation as him. He wanted to put away the right guys and not the wrong ones. He told her how he wanted to make a difference in the world. At that time, Brittany didn't think he meant what he said but standing next to her husband now she was one proud wife. Michael must have noticed that she was in la-la land because he pulled her closer to him and brought her back to the moment.

"Brittany and I wanted to talk to y'all about something. I know we should wait until later today to tell y'all but we really can't."

Brittany waited on him to finish his sentence so she would tell them the news.

"Like Michael said, we have something to tell y'all."

She made sure to make a dramatic pause. She almost laughed when she saw Taylor's face.

"We are going to have a baby!"

Taylor did a really good job at faking it. She even had

Brittany forgetting that she told her the news already. After Taylor calmed down, Mark came over and hugged Brittany. Everyone was all smiles and Michael was hugging Taylor and Mark. Taylor joined Mark and stood beside him just like before. Mark was the first one to speak.

"Well, you guys aren't the only ones with good news! We are having a baby too!"

Brittany did her best to act surprised. By the look on Taylor's face she pulled it off. Michael was silent and Brittany almost wondered if he already knew. When Michael finally opened his mouth, Brittany knew he didn't.

"Y'all are serious?"

Mark only nodded and shined a big goofy smile at Michael.

"I can't believe this! This is great news! Congratulations, y'all!"

Michael pulled Mark in for a hug while Brittany hugged Taylor. Mark moved past Michael and hugged Brittany while Taylor hugged Michael. By then, Taylor and Brittany were both in tears. Brittany was so happy and wanted to soak the memory in for as long as she could; especially with the lingering worry about Michael being in danger all over again. Just as the thought about Michael begin shooting moved through her brain, she heard his phone ring. Michael excused himself and went to answer it away from everyone. He was only gone a few seconds and then he returned.

"Briggs is at the front door. He must have knocked, but we couldn't hear him. He has some things he wants to go over with me. Y'all can join if y'all want to."

Brittany looked at Mark and Taylor, who's smiles all faded with hers. Brittany hoped it was good news because she didn't want anything to spoil their day. Everyone followed Michael inside.

Michael let Briggs in the house and had him follow him to the living room. Michael sat on the couch next to Brittany, and Taylor sat on the floor between Mark's legs. Briggs stood in the middle of the room and faced Michael.

"I came by to tell you what we have so far."

Michael nodded and waited for Briggs to find his words. Michael couldn't tell by Biggs' expression if the news was bad or good yet. He was the only person that Michael had a problem reading. Briggs was a person that never showed emotion on his face.

"We found out a few things, but not much to go on. The sketch you gave us hasn't turned anyone up yet and we are guessing that the girl wore a wig. We did manage to find a bullet out in the field near where your truck was. It must have hit your truck and landed in the bed of the truck but fell out when you flipped. Either way the bullet belonged to a twelve-gauge shot gun. We ran it through the data base but no hits came up to match any other shootings. We haven't found any witnesses yet and we don't think we will. I don't think she just walked there so we are trying to find where she parked her car. So far that's a dead end too."

Michael didn't feel any better about Briggs being there. It was eating him alive that someone tried to kill him. He dealt with his demons so there was no way it was about his past. Then the thought hit him that maybe it was someone he put away in the past.

"What about someone that I put away? Maybe they are coming after me now that they are out of jail or something?"

Briggs looked down at his shoes and said, "Michael, we thought about that but don't you think they would have made sure you were dead? The person fired two shots at your truck then ran off. If someone wanted to get you back for messing up their lives then they would have made sure you were dead."

Briggs does have a point.

"Okay, maybe you're right but what if they thought I would have died in the wreck? I almost did, but they could have watched me wreck and thought I wouldn't survive."

Briggs nodded his head.

"I go back to work Monday and I know I'm not supposed to be working until then, but bring me my files and I can go over them here at home. Don't even say no because there are way too many files for you to go over alone."

Briggs looked over at Brittany and waited for her to object but she didn't.

"Are you okay with this, Brittany?"

Brittany sighed and looked at Michael.

"I have to be because if I don't then he will just go up there and get them himself."

Michael let out a laugh and Briggs tried to hide his smile. Michael stood up because he thought it was the end of his meeting with Briggs.

"One more thing. I had the lab run the prints they found on the dead body of the girl you're helping. They were able to find something that suggests the prints might have been planted, but I have to run down there tomorrow and get more information from the techs. They also looked into Tiffany's cell phone log and she got a call around the time of the murder and the call pinged off a tower near her house."

Michael felt relief wash over him.

"I will keep in touch with you about what the techs say tomorrow and I'll bring the files by afterwards. I don't have anything planned after I bring you the files so I will hang around and help you dig through them."

Michael nodded and showed Briggs to the door. Once they were at the door, Michael stopped Briggs before he left.

"Look, does the boss think we have enough to cut Tiffany lose?"

Briggs stopped and looked at Michael.

"Right now, no, but when we get the information from the techs then yes we will have enough to let her go. The thing we are worried about is if she is being framed for this than she might end up dead."

Michael knew all too well what it felt like to be in Tiffany's shoes.

"Then we will get her some protection."

Briggs nodded and walked away. Michael closed the door and slowly felt his past coming back to haunt him. It was like he was replaying his situation all over again. However, he would make sure Tiffany didn't have to go through what he did to get her name cleared.

CHAPTER TEN

M ichael's cell phone rang early the next day. At first he didn't want to wake up to answer it. He looked to see who it was and what time it was. The phone flashed Briggs' number and in the corner of the phone the time read six thirty. Michael answered the phone and waited for Briggs to speak.

"Michael, I'm sorry to wake you up but I am heading to the lab to talk to the techs. Do you want to ride with me? This is our case and I know you would want to be there to ask questions. Just tell Brittany that you won't be doing anything but talking so no need to worry."

Michael sat up in the bed and looked over at Brittany who was now looking up at him.

"Of course, I want to go. I'll be ready in ten minutes so I'll meet you outside."

Brittany gave him a stern look and sat up in the bed with him. Michael knew he could potentially start a fight if he didn't think before he spoke.

"Baby, I am just going to ride with Briggs and talk to the techs. Then we are grabbing some files and coming back here."

Brittany rolled her eyes and pushed the covers back from her.

"Okay, Michael but if I find out that you are out there playing the role of Rambo, me and you will be fighting big time."

Brittany placed a soft kiss on his lips and then she went to the bathroom. Michael jumped up and threw on some casual clothes; after all he wasn't going into work. He ran downstairs and grabbed his house keys and wallet off the island in the kitchen, then was out the door to wait on Briggs.

Briggs pulled up about five minutes after Michael walked out on the porch to wait for him. Briggs didn't like much about his life and Michael guessed he had been that way since his dad passed away. The list of things Briggs did like was short but made Michael laugh. Briggs loved his truck, women, coffee, and his mom. Briggs treated his truck like a baby and washed it every weekend. Coffee and Briggs' mom went in the same category because he hated everyone else's coffee except for his moms. Then there was the way Briggs loved women and Michael found that one the funniest on the list. The funny thing about it was Briggs loved women, but women didn't love Briggs back. He always had a way of coming off too strong to women. Michael climbed up into Briggs's truck and buckled up.

Briggs had a nice truck. It was a black F350 with a lift kit on it. The inside was decked out in blue lights around the trim of the dash and doors. The lights went with the music that was playing. Michael laughed at the memory of when Briggs put them in. Michael and Briggs hadn't been partners long when Briggs asked Michael to help him hook up the radio and lights. Michael didn't know the first thing about running wires to a radio of a truck, but he agreed to help him anyway. Briggs did most of the work while Michael watched and learned how to do it.

When Briggs was almost done with the wiring, he faked

being shocked. Michael was lying in the floor looking up and letting Briggs know where to run the wires when Briggs yelled and started shaking. Michael jumped up and slammed his head into the dash of the truck and realized that Briggs was faking the whole thing because he was laughing. Briggs didn't let that go for two whole years. Briggs looked over at Michael and smiled.

"What's so funny, dude?"

Michael looked out the window.

"Just remembering when we hooked up the radio in the truck. I was glad you finally let it go but now I'm pretty sure it will be the topic of our lives."

Briggs laughed and they road in silence the rest of the way to the lab.

Briggs parked close to the door because the parking lot was mostly empty that day. It was Saturday so everyone who didn't have to work was home. Briggs and Michael got out and walked to the door. Once inside, they signed in and headed to the double doors where the lab techs were waiting on them. After walking in, Michael spotted a guy in a lab coat standing in the corner near the computer. Briggs cleared his throat so the guy wouldn't get scared by them walking in. The guy didn't turn around or make a move but he spoke quietly.

"Are y'all here to find out about the prints on Ms. Childress?"

Michael and Briggs walked closer to where the tech was standing and Briggs told the guy that they were there to find out about those prints.

The tech turned around and faced Michael and Briggs, then walked to a table where some papers were laying on it. He picked up a small stack of papers and handed them to

Michael.

"So, I have looked over the prints way too many times. I am going to try to explain what is telling me the prints are in fact planted. I missed it the last time and I am so glad y'all asked me to look at them again. So, your victim was stabbed in an over the head motion. Basically, the person was sitting on top of Ms. Childress when she was stabbed. The wounds on the victim were done in a downward motion that would require them to be in that position. That's not where I messed up though. When the suspect lifted Tiffany's prints off of a surface they planted them wrong. They planted them as if Tiffany stabbed the victim in an upward position."

The guy noticed Michael's face because he started speaking again.

"Here, let me show you the pictures of the internal wounds so you can see what I am talking about better."

The tech walked away and retuned a few minutes later with some pictures. The pictures showed Jennifer's body on the autopsy table. Protruding out of her body were stems showing the line of entry.

"You see this deep stab wound? The person had to stab her straight down. Now look at this picture of another stab wound where someone stabbed them in an upward position. See the difference?"

Michael and Briggs nodded. Each victims stab wounds were at a different angle.

"So, when your suspect planted the prints they planted them as if Tiffany stabbed your victim in an upward motion, but she didn't. The prints were placed in the wrong spots on the knife."

Michael felt relief wash over him because he knew that was enough to prove Tiffany didn't do it. Michael looked over at Briggs.

"Let's call the boss and get Tiffany out of jail now!"

Briggs laughed and followed Michael to the truck.

**

Tiffany had finally fallen asleep on her cot when she heard a door slam down the hall. She hadn't been able to sleep much since she was thrown in her cell. She still couldn't believe that everyone really thought she killed her own sister. Then again, she had all the reason to. Everyone saw the bad in their relationship and never the good. Tiffany was never really big into religion, but every night since she was arrested she had prayed that Michael would be able to prove her innocence. Tiffany sat up when she heard footsteps coming from down the hall and waited to see where they were going. She caught a glance at the cop and then looked down at her feet because she knew he would just keep on walking. Suddenly the footsteps stopped and Tiffany looked up to see where the cop was at. She saw him standing in front of her cell door playing with his keys. Tiffany jumped up because she thought that Michael was there to talk to her again. The cop unlocked the door and waited on Tiffany to walk out.

Tiffany stood at the door and waited on him to tell her she had a visitor, but he never said a word. Tiffany just walked out and waited on the cop to cuff her, but he didn't. She stood still and felt her nerves take over. Her legs began to shake just slightly and the hairs on her arms stood up with bumps all over her skin. She had no clue if it was good nerves or bad. Either way something was going on and she demanded to know what.

"What's going on, officer?"

The cop cleared his throat and grabbed her arm.

"Officer Sims is here to speak with you."

That was all he said before he began to walk down the hall towards the interview room. He opened the door and walked out leaving her standing in the room alone.

The door on the opposite side opened and Michael walked in with a smile on his face.

"Sit down Tiffany because we need to talk."

Tiffany could feel the air change around her. She knew there was some news about everything going on and she was dying to know. Tiffany sat down in front of Michael in the chair and waited for him to talk.

"Tiffany, you are a free woman. We found some evidence to prove you didn't kill your sister."

Tiffany stopped listening to anything else he said because at that moment she heard the words she never thought she would hear. She was a free woman and they had the proof they needed. She could tell Michael was still talking, but wasn't sure what he was saying because the shock hadn't left her body yet. Tiffany could feel her eyes blinking rapidly and a flutter ping through her stomach. She finally was able to find her voice and speak, but when she did it was more of a squeak.

"I'm free."

Tiffany realized that Michael wasn't talking anymore and felt a little embarrassed that she had zoned out like she did. When she looked up at Michael, he was smiling at her and studying her face.

"Tiffany, have you been listening to me at all?"

Tiffany shook her head and started to play with her hands.

"I'll start over again, okay?"

Tiffany nodded her head in agreement and looked into his eyes so he would know she was paying attention.

"My partner and I were able to prove your finger prints were in fact planted on the murder weapon. It wasn't easy and our lab techs missed it the first time around, which explains why you were charged in the first place. We are worried that once you are free and it hits headlines that you're not the killer, the killer may come for you."

There was a knock at the door. Michael stopped talking and waited for the person to enter. Tiffany's eyes left Michael's and went to the door and found the man who walked in. He was very handsome and had an edgy look to him. She felt her head spin a little and her mouth even fell open slightly.

He had on khaki pants and a button up blue shirt. His hair was light brown with a red tint to it. She never thought of a man in so much detail before and it felt weird for her to notice so much about him. The man sat a stack of papers in front of Michael and looked right at her. She felt like he was looking through her soul. Her hands even started to shake and she could feel her eyes move from him to other spots in the room. She couldn't bring herself to look him in the eyes for a long period of time because when she did it felt wrong. Michael spoke and her eyes found his immediately.

"This is my partner, Officer Briggs. Briggs this is Tiffany Childress."

He smiled again at her and said hey in a deep voice. Tiffany could only smile right then because her brain didn't work well enough to tell her mouth to talk. She looked back to Michael and waited for him to speak again.

"Like I was saying before, you aren't safe right now. We

will have protection for you until we catch whoever did this to you and your sister. We know it can be stressful to have someone follow you all the time or staying with you, but we promise it is for your safety. If someone was willing to frame you then they will be willing to try to murder you once they know you're free. Do you still not have any clue who would want to murder your sister and frame you?"

Tiffany didn't know anyone that would want to kill her sister, let alone frame her. Right then she just wanted to get out of that shit hole and go home. All she could do was shake her head no. Briggs walked over closer to where she was sitting.

"It's short notice to have someone stay with you right now so for the weekend, I will be staying with you and when Monday rolls around we will have someone else come sit with you."

Tiffany could only nod her head because she was embarrassed and worried that he noticed her nervousness towards him. Briggs stood up and walked back towards the door as Michael followed him.

"Come on, Tiffany. Let's get you out of here and home, okay?"

Tiffany stood up and followed both men to freedom with her stomach flipping in excitement.

CHAPTER ELEVEN

B riggs looked over in the seat beside him and saw Tiffany looking out the window. She hadn't said much since they left the station, but he understood why. If it wasn't for Michael, she might have been stuck in jail for the rest of her life. Briggs knew that he shouldn't say anything, but he needed to break the silence. They had just dropped Michael off at home and they were headed to Briggs' house for him to get some clothes.

"Feels good to be out, doesn't it?"

Tiffany looked over at him and he felt his heart pick up speed for the second time that day.

"It really does. I don't think I could have made it in there. Thanks again to you and your partner. I know I will say it a thousand more times, but I can't thank you both enough."

Briggs didn't know what it was, but when she spoke, his life stood still. He always had a thing for women but women never had a thing for him. Michael always said he came off too strong, but that was just the type of guy he was. He knew he couldn't get close to Tiffany because she was a part of the case and his chief would have his ass. He had to control whatever urges his head and heart had. It was business and he intended to keep it that way. He had to keep her safe from whoever was lurking in the dark.

"We are almost to my house. I just have to run in and get some stuff so when we get there feel free to make yourself at home until I'm ready to go."

Tiffany smiled at him and went back to looking out the window.

Briggs pulled up to his house and parked his truck in the driveway. He lived in a small house near town, but off the road just enough to be private. Tiffany jumped out of the truck, shut the door and followed him to the door.

"Don't pay attention to the mess. I'm hardly ever home thanks to my job."

Tiffany nodded and waited on him to unlock the door. Briggs caught a glimpse of Tiffany looking over her shoulder off into the woods. She had to have been worried about someone possibly trying to kill her. He planned to make sure she was safe at all cost. He didn't know if that was his job history talking or his heart, but either way she would be safe.

***

Tiffany watched Briggs open the door. He let her walk in first. She couldn't help but almost run in the house because she got a weird feeling someone was watching her. She knew she was being framed, but she never knew someone would try to kill her if they couldn't frame her. She was over one hump and now she had to get over another one. She didn't know why, but she felt safe with Briggs around. Her mind kept telling her it was because she was attracted to him, but she made sure to push that thought out quickly. She needed to find out who killed her sister and not get involved with a cop.

Briggs had a beautiful house that made her think he had a woman in his life. Everything had a place and was put away neatly. The only thing that seemed to be missing was pictures on the walls. Tiffany stood in the living room and looked around her. She felt out of place and didn't know what to do so she stood there awkwardly. Briggs spoke and made her jump.

"You can have a seat on the couch. It won't take but a second. Do you want anything to drink? I have Dr. Pepper, sweet tea, and water."

Tiffany shook her head no and sat down on the couch.

The two rooms that she could see were big in size. The living room and kitchen were both open to each other and there was one door in the living room. Briggs went into that door and shut it behind him. Tiffany saw some magazines on the stand next to her and she picked them up. There were two and both were shopping catalogs for police supplies. She thumbed through them both quickly not paying attention to anything she saw. Her mind was in a whole other place at that time and she couldn't shake the bad feeling she had. As she sat the magazines back down on the table, the door opened and she jumped again. Briggs walked out of the door with a duffle bag in his hand. He smiled at her and she felt her heart start beating fast again. She flashed a grin at him because at that time that was all she could manage. He stopped where she was sitting and waited on her to stand up.

"Are you okay? You are a little jumpy and you don't look so good."

Tiffany didn't know how to take what he was asking. She had felt a little offended, but brushed it off.

"I'm okay. I'm a little worried and everything is moving really fast."

He nodded his head and walked to the front door. Tiffany followed behind him and once he opened the door she practically ran out of it to the truck.

***

Briggs couldn't help but admire the way she walked towards the truck. With every steep she took, he felt his eyes follow. She dang near ran to the truck and he felt a little sad for her. He knew she was safe right then and hated she was so worried. She was more than jumpy It was like every noise scared the hell out of her. He walked to the truck with his bag in hand and threw it in the back seat. He jumped in the driver seat and started the truck. Tiffany was already buckled and waiting for him. He pulled onto the road and started his way to her house.

Briggs pulled up to Tiffany's house and parked his truck behind her car in the driveway. She had a nice house with a warm feeling to it. Tiffany was out of the truck and walking up the sidewalk to the front door. Briggs jumped out of the truck and ran to catch up to her. He grabbed her arm and pulled her back so she would stop walking.

"Did you forget that someone might be trying to kill you?"

She looked at him with an angry look and then it turned into a confused face.

"What does that have to do with anything?"

He let her arm go and looked down at his feet.

"I have to check the house out first before you go in. I need to make sure no one is inside or anything could hurt you."

Tiffany folded her arms over each other and let them rest on her chest. He rolled his eyes and walked to the front door. He looked around the door to see if anything looked out of the ordinary.

"I need your house keys, Tiffany."

Tiffany walked around the corner to where he was standing and threw the keys at him. That time she rolled her eyes at him before walking back around the corner. Briggs noticed the trim around the door was missing where the frame was at. He thought at first that maybe she had a new door put in. Briggs put the key in the door and turned the lock. He heard the lock click and then a slight beeping sound.

"Tiffany, run now!" Briggs said as he let go of the handle and ran dropping the keys.

He looked at Tiffany's eyes as she started running down the driveway. Briggs wasn't far behind her with his heart beating out of his chest. He could be wrong, but that beep didn't sound like it was supposed to be there. Just as the thought hit his mind there was a blast that knocked him into Tiffany. They both landed on the ground on their stomachs. The house was in flames and glass flew all around them. Briggs used his body to shield Tiffany from the glass and wood flying around them. He felt a sharp burning in his side, but he didn't care. All that mattered at that time was that Tiffany was okay. After everything stopped flying around, Briggs tried to stand up but couldn't, so he just rolled off Tiffany onto the ground.

He looked over at Tiffany and she wasn't moving. He reached over and put two fingers to her neck and felt her pulse. She was knocked out, probably from the fall. She had a few cuts on her arms and one on her head, but overall he figured she was okay. He looked down at his legs to see why he couldn't stand. Sticking out of his leg was a piece of glass that came from a window. He reached in his back pocket hoping to find his phone. Once he got it, he dialed 9-1-1 and waited for them to answer. He looked over at Tiffany's house and saw it in flames. People were coming outside of their homes and screaming. Briggs laid back down on the ground and felt everything around him start to spin. He didn't want to close his eyes because he needed to protect Tiffany, but his body had other plans for him. Slowly, everything went dark and Briggs passed out.

CHAPTER TWELVE

Tiffany woke up on a stretcher with a mask on her face. She looked over and saw Briggs laying on one next to her. She sat up, took off the mask, and looked around at what was going on. There were fire trucks, police cars, ambulances, and people everywhere. She smelled smoke and heard people shouting around her. Someone touched Tiffany's arm and she jumped. It was Michael.

"Are you okay?"

Tiffany confusedly nodded her head. Then it all came back to her. Her house blew up and Briggs saved her.

"How is Briggs?"

Michael looked over at the other stretcher where Briggs was laying.

"He's okay. He had a piece of glass in his leg, but they got it out and stitched it up. He had a few more cuts and they cleaned those up. He did get hit on the head and knocked out. We are guessing that's what happened to you too."

Tiffany looked down at her arms. They were both cut up, but not hurting badly, and she was dirty. She figured it was from landing on the ground. She got down off the stretcher and went to where Briggs was laying.

"He saved my life. He jumped on me when the blast happened and kept me from getting hurt. I owe him my life."

Tiffany squeezed Briggs hand and turned to look at the house.

"What about my cat? Did they manage to get the cat out?"

Michael looked over his shoulder and then back to her.

"Yeah. Someone got the cat and took it to the vet. They said you should be able to pick it up tomorrow."

She sucked in a breath and let it out slowly. The house was being put out with fire hoses and smoke rolled off the roof. She looked back up at Michael.

"Who would do this to me?"

Michael looked down at Briggs and back at her.

"I don't know, Tiffany, but I plan to find out. Once Briggs wakes up, I'm sending you both to a safe house. I don't know if they will try to hurt him too, but I'm not taking the chance."

Michael didn't give her a chance to argue before he walked away. She didn't want to go to a safe house. She wanted to go home. She looked back at her house and knew that was out of the question. She pulled her stretcher closer to Briggs and sat down on it. She wanted to be there to thank him once he woke up.

***

Once Briggs woke up and felt okay to walk, they rode to the police station to get everything settled. Tiffany sat next to Briggs in what she guessed was a cafeteria and watched him drink some coffee. Neither one of them spoke since they had gotten to the station and Tiffany was okay with that. She heard footsteps and turned to see who it was. Michael and an older man walked up to where they were sitting.

"Tiffany, this is mine and Briggs' boss Chief Belue. We need to talk to y'all about a few things."

Tiffany watched Michael pull up two chairs and sat at the table with them.

"Briggs, when you got to Tiffany's house did you notice anything out of place? Cars, people, or anything?" Michael asked.

Tiffany looked at Briggs and waited for him to speak. He was deep in thought and Tiffany wasn't sure if he was ever going to answer Michael.

"I saw a black car parked down the street when we pulled in but I didn't see anyone inside it. Then at the front door, I noticed the strip that goes around the frame was missing. I figured Tiffany had a new door put in or something. It wasn't until I heard a slight beep when I unlocked the door that I knew there was a bomb."

Briggs closed his eyes like he was trying to remember something.

"There was a person walking down the street with a backpack on! Why didn't I notice it before now?"

Michael looked over to Chief Belue who said, "Don't beat yourself up, Briggs. Sometimes we don't notice things like that right off the bat. Tiffany, do you remember anything?"

Tiffany sat up straight and looked down at her hands folded in her lap.

"No, I never noticed the car or person walking. I was so focused on getting in my house that I almost went in before

Briggs. He stopped me and kept me from going in. He saved my life today and we got lucky."

Michael patted Briggs on the back and smiled.

"Yes, you both are lucky and it's all thanks to Briggs. Here is the thing. We think that whoever tried to kill me and shot my truck is the same person that tried to kill y'all today. Someone found out that I was trying to get Tiffany out of jail and prove she was framed. Then when you helped Tiffany out by protecting her today, they tried to kill you both. None of us are safe until we find out who this is. You can't stay at your house, Briggs, they probably know where you live and due to today you can't stay at Tiffany's house. I'm not even safe at my own house to be honest. That's why we are all going to stick together. You, Tiffany, Brittany and I are all going to stay at our place. We will have around the clock guards and won't go out in public unless we all are together. This is better then what everyone else wanted us to do. Trust me."

Tiffany knew he was talking about witness protection. She didn't like the thought of being at someone else's house, but it was better than being in a different state and wiped off the face of the earth. Briggs didn't seem to care much by the look on his face. The decision was made and Tiffany was okay with it. Michael and Briggs talked a little longer with their boss and then got up to leave. Tiffany followed and kept to herself. She felt so alone in all of it and wished she had family or friends to talk to.

***

Briggs and Tiffany pulled up to Michael's house. They had another cop escort them to get some of their stuff. Tiffany didn't have much because the explosion wiped out most of her things. Briggs felt like it was his fault. He knew something was off, but he shrugged off the signs. He tried to shake the thought from his mind and got out of the truck.

Tiffany was already out and reaching for her bag in the back seat. He reached over and grabbed it before she could. It was the least he could do, since she'd just lost everything she had worked for and was having to stay with complete strangers. Tiffany pulled her hand back fast and shut the door. She walked around to the front of the truck and waited for him to walk up on the porch first.

Briggs limped up the porch. Before he could reach the door it swung open. Brittany and Michael stood in the doorway waiting for them.

"Let me help you with your bags, Briggs."

Michael walked out and took a bag from Briggs. He looked over his shoulder and saw Tiffany with her arms crossed walking up to the porch. Briggs decided to give her some space and would talk to her alone later. After walking into Michael and Brittany's home, Briggs set his bag down next to Tiffany's at the door way. Briggs loved their home because of the feeling it gave off. It was a country feel but also had a touch of the city life. He walked down the hall and followed Brittany and Michael into their living room. Brittany sat in a chair on one side of the room and Tiffany sat down on the couch. Michael stood near the opening of the room so Briggs decided to sit with Tiffany. Brittany was the first one to break the silence.

"We only have one extra bed right now because the spare room is currently my office. We are planning to add onto the house soon, but it will take some time. For now, one of you can take the bedroom and the other will have to take the couch. We also have an air mattress, so if one of you is okay with sleeping on it then you can. If you decided to take the air mattress, I'll blow it up and put it in the room. Also, please make yourselves at home. There is soda, beer, food, and tea in the fridge. The bathroom is down the hall and is stocked up with everything y'all would need. Tiffany, I also put some of my soap and shampoo in there in case you didn't have any."

Briggs looked over at Tiffany and for the first time that day she smiled.

"Thank you so much for doing that. After the blast, there wasn't much left."

Tiffany looked down at her hands and they were shaking. Briggs wanted to get her alone and make sure she was okay. He almost reached for her hand to stop it from shaking, but he held back.

Tiffany cleared her throat and started talking again, "I don't want to be a bother being here and I feel awful about it. If there is anything I can do, please tell me."

Brittany nodded her head and grabbed Michael's hand. Briggs was glad Michael had Brittany. Michael could be like the hulk at times and Brittany knew how to calm him down. Briggs almost laughed at his next thought of Michael not ever being able to calm Brittany down when she was riled up. Brittany was feisty.

"I know you two have to be tired, so I'll let y'all settle in. Once y'all get settled then come to the kitchen and I'll fix y'all some food."

Brittany smiled at Briggs and Tiffany then walked towards the kitchen. Michael followed not far behind her. Briggs got up and headed to the room that was attached to the living room. Tiffany wasn't far behind him when he entered.

"I'll take the couch so you can take the bed. I don't want to disturb you and you need your sleep."

Briggs went to the bed, grabbed a pillow, and turned to walked back out. He didn't make it to the door when he heard Tiffany say, "No, you can use the air mattress and put it at the end of the bed. As long as you don't mind my snoring."

Tiffany flashed a smile and Briggs turned stopped.

"As long as you're sure then I guess that would be okay. Oh, and don't worry, I snore too."

Briggs set the pillow back on the bed and walked to the door.

"I'm going to go grab our bags and I'll be right back."

Briggs grabbed the bags and walked back to the bedroom. Tiffany was sitting on the bed facing the wall and crying. When she heard him walk in, she wiped her face and sat up straight. Briggs knew she was hurting. She lost her house, lost her sister, and someone was after her.

"Tiffany, do you mind if I sit with you and talk to you for a second?"

Tiffany sniffled a little and shrugged her shoulders. Briggs took that as a yes so he sat down next to her.

"I know this is a lot to take in right now. You lost your house and that can't be easy, but you're alive. You should be grateful that you're alive. We will find who did this and they will pay for what they have done. You just have to trust me, okay?"

Tiffany started to cry again and Briggs decided to embrace her in a hug. She hesitated at first, but then pulled him closer to her and really started to sob. Briggs decided to just hold her and let her get it all out. She needed someone and she didn't have anyone in her family left. He would just have to be that someone for her for a while. Briggs took a hand and ran it through her hair to help calm her. His heart broke with her at that moment.

CHAPTER THIRTEEN

T iffany stepped into the shower and washed away the dried up blood and ash from the fire. The hot water felt good on her body. Her mind drifted to the events that happened that day. She didn't want to think about it, but it seemed to keep coming back to her mind. She was so grateful that Briggs was with her when the blast happened. He risked his life to save her. She felt her heart pick up speed at the thought of Briggs. She felt the same feeling the first time she saw him and then again at his house.

When he was lying on the stretcher hurt, she almost lost it. She knew she had feelings for him, but she refused to show them to him. *Maybe he feels the same way, but is afraid to show it?* She pushed the thought aside as fast as it came to her. Tiffany put her hands on the shower wall and let the water spray her on the face. Briggs told her everything was going to be alright, but she didn't know how anything could possibly be okay. She was scared she was going to die and everyone trying to help her was going to die too. She reached down and shut the water off and wished the thoughts away.

Tiffany felt much better after having a shower and some food. Brittany made subs and they had beer. Tiffany didn't realize how hungry she was until she took a bite of her sub. She ended up eating all of it and drinking four beers. She felt more relaxed then she thought she could with everything going on. Michael and Brittany went upstairs to their room once they ate dinner. Tiffany washed her plate and went to her room. She wondered where Briggs was and even asked Brittany. Brittany had told her he ate and went to the room. She guessed he was just tired from everything he had dealt with that day.

Tiffany opened the door to the room and found Briggs on an air mattress in the floor at the end of the bed. He had a lap top opened and was sitting up with a stern look on his face. Tiffany slowly walked in and went to the bed. She didn't want to disturb him from whatever he was doing. She reached the bed and just as she was about to get in she heard him clear his throat.

"Are you going to bed, Tiffany?"

Tiffany stood back up and looked around the bed to see him.

"Yeah, I was going to try and get some sleep. You can keep working; it won't bother me at all. I usually sleep like a rock so it's really okay."

She could see his face from the light on the computer screen. She caught a glimpse of his shoulders and realized that he wasn't wearing a shirt. She never thought he would have the muscles that he did. His neck and shoulders were cut and tight looking. Her heart picked up speed and she caught him looking at her. Her hands started to sweat, and she felt the hairs on her arms sticking up. It was crazy how much of an effect he had on her. It was like he could see right through her into her soul.

"I was actually heading to bed also. I just need to run to the bath room really fast and then you won't hear a peep out of me the rest of the night."

She saw him smile and she smiled back. Tiffany cut the

lamp on the side table on. Briggs scooted off the mattress and closed his lap top. As he stood up, Tiffany couldn't take her eyes off him. With the light was shining on his body, she could see that he was indeed built. His stomach was every bit of a six pack, even though she didn't take the time to count his abs. He had on basketball shorts that hung on his hips in just the right way. Her favorite part of his body was the line that started from the front of his hips and went up his stomach. She looked back up his body to his face and saw him looking at her. She quickly looked away and felt her face turn red. She looked down at her hands and started to fidget with them.

"Sorry, I didn't mean to stare at you. That was rude of me."

She heard him laugh under his breath and softly whisper to her, "It's okay, Tiffany."

When she turned around, he was closing the door behind him. She took that as a good time to change into something more comfortable. She was going to sleep in shorts and a shirt, but she knew too many clothes would bother her. She walked to where her bag was sitting on the floor and found her robe and a silk, black nightie. She laid them both on the bed and started to get dressed.

***

Briggs splashed some water on his face and looked in the mirror. He was worried about Tiffany's safety and wondered if he would ever catch whoever was after her. None of it made any sense and to make things worse he couldn't find Tiffany's mother. It was like she fell of the face of the earth and Briggs was worried she just might have. He was starting to think she was dead somewhere and no one knew it. Either way, finding her was going to be extremely hard.

Briggs walked out of the bathroom and let his eyes adjust to the darkness. Once he could make out where everything was in the dark, he walked to the room. He opened the door and immediately felt bad for not knocking. Tiffany was standing near the bed in nothing but panties, trying to slip her nightie on over her head. Briggs breath caught in his throat and his eyes couldn't leave her body. His body started to feel warm and his urge to touch her became stronger. She turned and faced him and he still couldn't look away. She had caught him looking so there wasn't a point in hiding it. His body was stiff and his feet were planted in that spot. He didn't know what to say or do so he just shut the door and turned back to face her. She stood staring at him for what seemed like hours and he stared back at her.

Her hair was down and damp. He even noticed something different about her eyes that made his body respond. He had to look away or else he was going to regret it. He looked down at his feet and finally spoke.

"I'm sorry, I should have knocked."

He looked back up at Tiffany and she slipped on her robe.

"It's okay. I should have told you I was going to change."

She closed her robe and sat on the bed. Briggs walked to his bed and smiled at her.

"You know, it was only fair. I did catch you staring at me earlier so count it as pay back."

Tiffany's mouth fell open, but no words came out. He wanted to laugh out loud, but he decided to leave it at that. He laid down on the bed and covered up. She must have been in shock because she didn't move or say anything for a few minutes. Briggs decided to break the ice and save her some embarrassment.

"Hey Tiffany, can you turn off that light?"

Just as soon as he said it the light went out and he heard her climb into bed. He let a quiet laugh escape and rolled over on his side. It took some time, but he finally fell asleep.

***

"I don't understand how the fuck they didn't die. That bitch and her new found boyfriend should have died in the explosion. I planted everything perfect and even stayed back to watch her die. She was supposed to open the door first, but he just had to step in and save the day. I saw him dive on top of her and hoped something landed on them, killing them both. Just my luck it didn't and now I have to plan everything all over again. I will get her and she will pay for all the shit she put me through. All these years she had no idea I was right there under her nose. Her stupid sister found out the hard way just how mad I was. Now it's her turn to find out. I have to get her alone and it has to be soon! Then again, I could just kill them all and walk away. No one even knows I exist so what would it even matter. I need to think this through and get it right this time. I'm done dealing with this shit and I'm done looking at their stupid faces."

***

Tiffany was having a bad dream. Her body shook from side to side and sweat was running all over her body. She tried to wake up, but neither her mind nor body would let her. In the dream her house blew up over and over, but she was trapped inside when it did. Briggs was outside watching the whole time and his eyes were the last thing she saw before it started over again. Tiffany felt shaking and she finally woke up. She looked around the room and remembered where she was at. Briggs was standing over her with a worried look on his face. She looked down and realized her whole body was still shaking.

"Tiffany, are you okay? Looks like you were having a nightmare and a pretty bad one at that."

"Yeah, I think I'm okay. It was so real and so bad."

Briggs turned and walked out of the room. She felt a little mad that he would just up and leave her right then. He must not care about her like she thought he did. Her mind shut up once she saw him rush back in, shut the door, and climb in bed next to her. She was speechless.

"Here is a cold wash rag for you. Wipe your head so you can cool off. That must have been a bad nightmare because you were screaming."

Tiffany didn't know she screamed, but she knew the dream was enough to keep her wide awake now. Once she caught her breath, she looked over at Briggs.

"Thank you for waking me up. If I would have stayed in that nightmare I'm not sure how crazy I would have been when I did wake up."

Briggs smiled at her and she felt her body relax.

"You mean you can get even crazier then you are now?"

Tiffany let out a laugh and it made her feel much better. Briggs stood up and headed for his mattress on the floor. Tiffany felt her heart start beating fast again and her breath getting quicker. She was scared and didn't want to sleep alone. Before she could think, she said, "Please don't leave me."

She wished the words back as soon as they were out. He stopped dead in his tracks and gave a weird look.

"Are you sure it's okay?"

Tiffany only nodded because she still couldn't believe

what she had just asked him. He walked back to the bed and laid down next to her. He didn't touch her, but just having him so close to her made her body want to touch him. She controlled her urge and eventually fell back to sleep.

CHAPTER FOURTEEN

Briggs didn't think he would ever fall asleep because his brain didn't want to shut up. He knew sleeping in the same bed with Tiffany was wrong, but yet there he was. It felt different for him to sleep in a bed with someone. His experience with women usually wasn't good and if a woman was in his bed they weren't there to sleep. They were always gone before sleep ever became a thought. He liked having Tiffany next to him, which was a surprise to him. He still couldn't fall asleep and even thought about getting back on the air mattress. He pushed the covers back and rolled over on his back. The movement he made must have startled Tiffany because she rolled over on her side that faced him. He didn't move because he was worried she would wake up. Briggs wanted her to get as much sleep as she could because he knew she really needed it.

Tiffany made a whimpering noise, then scooted closer to his side and wrapped her arm around his stomach. Briggs didn't know what to do but his mind was ringing with alarms. He needed to move her off him, but he knew she would wake up. Deep down he didn't want her to move. He even thought about turning over and pulling her closer to him. He felt a comfortable feeling wash over him and his mind finally shut down. He rolled over to face her and pulled the covers back over him. He wanted to enjoy the moment because he planned to not let it happen again. He lifted his hand and brushed her hair from her face. Tiffany let out a breath and scooted up against his chest. Briggs wrapped his arm around her and played with her hair. He finally closed his eyes. Within minutes, Briggs was asleep holding Tiffany in his arms.

***

Michael woke up to the sound of Brittany getting sick in the bathroom. He jumped up and ran to the bathroom. He found Brittany on the floor hugging the toilet. He reached over, grabbed a rag and wet it with cold water. He slid down in the floor beside Brittany and moved her hair from her face.

"Here baby, use this rag. It'll help."

Brittany took the rag without looking up at him.

"Michael, I am tired of getting sick all day every day."

Michael wished he could take it all away from her. He would give anything to be sick so she didn't have to be. He stood up and helped Brittany to her feet. Once she was stable, he walked to the bath tub. He ran water in the tub and added bubbles. When he turned around Brittany was standing at the sink.

"Do you think they will be okay, baby?"

It took Michael a second to figure out what she was talking about.

"Yeah, I do. They are really strong plus, they are here so of course they are okay."

Michael felt a burning in his stomach from the words. He told Mark and Taylor they would all be okay, but in the end they almost died. He would never forgive himself for what happened to Taylor and Mark. Michael watched Brittany pull off her clothes and step into the bath tub. He loved how Brittany's body was changing. It wasn't enough to notice with clothes on but he could tell when she was naked. Her skin felt different and her stomach poked out just a tiny bit. He figured he was just seeing things since she wasn't that far along. He shook his head and walked back to the bedroom.

The clock on the nightstand showed that it was six-thirty. He figured sleep wasn't coming back to him, so he decided to get a head start on his day. He planned on having some officers bring over some case files so he and Briggs could work from home. He threw on some clothes and headed down stairs. Once in the kitchen, he started coffee and got food out to cook. He figured French toast and eggs would be good enough for everyone. He knew Brittany probably wouldn't eat because of the baby. It had gotten hard to get her to eat anything, so he would leave her alone. Plus, she was already sick and he didn't want her to feel worse. Michael went to work fixing breakfast with the case and Brittany on his mind.

***

Tiffany woke up with the sun shining in the window near the bed. She felt better than she did the day before. She blinked and tried to focus her eyes on her surroundings. She looked next to her and saw Briggs lying on his side facing her. He was still asleep and a lot closer then she remembered him being the night before. She tried to move her arm and realized his arm was laying over hers. He was cuddling with her. She was in shock until she figured out she was cuddling with him just as much as he was with her. She had her leg over his and was almost nose to nose with him. She slowly moved her arm and tried not to wake him up. Her eyes grew bigger with every move she made. She almost had her arm out from under his but his eyes opened. Her heart froze and she felt more embarrassed then she ever knew she could.

She looked into his eyes and waited for him to fully understand the situation. He pulled his arm back and rubbed his eyes.

"I slept like a rock once I finally fell asleep. Did you cuddle with me?"

He was looking at her smiling and she still couldn't move or speak. She pulled her leg from his and inched her way back to her side of the bed.

"Sorry about that. I honestly don't remember any of it."

Briggs laughed and rolled over on his back.

"Tiffany, you act like we had sex. It's seriously okay and we both finally got some sleep. Think of it as a good thing. I made you feel safe and you helped me fill an empty hole."

She watched his face, looking for a sign that he was upset about sleeping with her. There weren't any signs of him being upset. She decided to let it go and get on with her day.

"Well, I'm going to go get ready for my day. Do you want to use the bathroom first? I might be a while so I don't want to keep you waiting."

He smiled at her and said, "Sure, I won't be but a second."

He jumped out of bed and slid his shorts on over his boxers. She didn't remember him taking his shorts off. Either way she noticed his nice firm butt. She made sure to look away before he noticed. Once he walked out of the room, she gathered her things together. She needed to get on the right track to finding her sister's killer and the horrible person who tried to frame her.

***

Briggs walked out of the room and headed to the bathroom. He instantly smelled food coming from the kitchen. He figured it must have been Brittany cooking, but to his surprise it was Michael. He stopped in the hall before heading into the bathroom.

"Hey dude, you okay? You look like your dog died."

Michael put some eggs on a plate and turned to face Briggs.

"Yeah, man, I'm okay. It's a lot to explain right now. Plus, I need Britt around to tell everyone anyway."

Briggs stood there with a confused look on his face.

"Dude, just get ready, Britt and I will explain it when you sit down to eat."

Reluctantly Briggs headed to the bathroom and got ready. Once he was done, he knocked on the room door and told Tiffany that he was done with the bathroom. He walked back to the kitchen and sat down at the table. He didn't want to bother Michael while he cooked; he just wanted a minute to gather his thoughts. He knew sleeping with Tiffany was a bad idea. He couldn't figure out why he decided to wrap his arms around her. Then it didn't help the she didn't seem to be happy about it when she woke up. He slept better than he ever had before, but he knew not to make a habit of it. He refused to let his feelings get in the way of the case. Michael made that mistake before and almost lost everyone he loved. Michael walked over with a tray of food and drinks. Briggs put on a smile. He didn't want Michael to know he had feelings for Tiffany. Besides, Michael had something to tell him and he was interested to know what it was.

***

Brittany walked down the stairs and heard everyone talking in the kitchen. She smelt food and almost ran back upstairs to the bathroom to get sick again. She loved the thought of having a baby, but being sick was taking a toll on her body. She was gaining weight and she couldn't figure out how. She never ate because she felt so sick all the time. She pushed the thoughts aside and went into the kitchen. Everyone was at the bar talking about the case. Michael noticed her first and walked to where she was standing. Briggs looked over at her and smiled. Tiffany looked at her and back to Briggs. Brittany had a feeling that Tiffany and Briggs had feelings for each other, but were fighting it because of the circumstances. Brittany smiled and held Michael's hand. Michael pulled her close to him. Briggs laughed and spoke up.

"I was so right! Can I please say I told you so?"

Brittany was confused. Michael laughed and looked down at her.

"We are having a baby. We haven't told many people. In fact, we only told our friends and the two of you. We plan on telling our family this weekend."

Briggs busted out laughing and Michael laughed at him.

Brittany looked up at Michael and asked, "What's so funny?"

"Well, the day you were sick and refused to go to the doctor, Briggs said you were pregnant. Since he was right he is going to rub it in my face until I admit it."

Brittany laughed and looked at Briggs and said, "Well, you were right."

They all sat down at the table. The morning was spent talking about the baby. It was good for Briggs and Tiffany to briefly take their minds off of her case and Brittany and Michael enjoyed talking about their bundle of joy.

Luckily, Brittany felt better by lunch time. Briggs and Michael were in the office working on the case and Tiffany was curled up on the couch talking on her phone. Brittany decided to fix herself something to eat. She went to work making some tea and chopped up some fruit. She couldn't think of anything else she really wanted to eat. Tea seemed to help her stomach settle down and the fruit was easier coming back up. She pulled the tea pot off the stove and heard footsteps. She turned, poured her tea in the cup, and looked up to see Tiffany standing there.

Tiffany was a beautiful girl she just wore the worry on her face. Brittany could see the pain that everything had caused in her eyes.

"Would you like some hot tea?"

Tiffany smiled and nodded her head.

"I am so sorry about your sister and your house. I know that's not going to make any of it better but I wanted you to know I'm here if you need to talk."

"Thank you. I just got off the phone with the insurance company and they are sending a contractor out to see if my house is fixable. As for my sister, I still have to go get her stuff out of her house and pick up her cat. I can't get over everything that's happened. It's all been so fast and one thing after another. First my sister dies, then I'm arrested for her murder, then my house blows up, and someone tries to kill me. The part that I can't wrap my head around is the fact that it has all happened within a few weeks. How can my life fall apart in such a short amount of time?"

Brittany felt her heart break for Tiffany. She really wished there was something she could do for her.

"If you want, I can help you get your sisters stuff. I can only imagine how hard it is going through all of it. I can also help you when you have to deal with the insurance claims and the insurance adjuster. Trust me; you will have to deal with them more than once."

Tiffany smiled and Brittany could tell it was a genuine smile.

"I would really like the help. It's harder than I thought it would be especially dealing with the house too. I just want it all to go away."

Brittany nodded. She was glad to be a friend of Tiffany's and even happier that Tiffany was talking to her.

CHAPTER FIFTEEN

Tiffany walked out onto the porch. She decided to sit on the swing that was hanging from the roof of the porch. She took a sip of her tea and looked around the yard. It was truly a beautiful place that Michael and Brittany had. Tiffany couldn't get over how quiet it was. She was used to living in a subdivision and people were always around her. The only thing around her right then was birds and squirrels. She took a deep breath and thought back to when she was a little girl. She remembered a time when her mom made her pancakes for breakfast and Jennifer got upset that she used all the syrup. Her dad ran out to the store and picked up some for them. Jennifer didn't talk to her for a whole week over the syrup.

No matter how much Tiffany tried to think, she couldn't figure out who would want her and her sister dead. Tiffany never made anyone mad or hate her. She had no clue if her sister had anyone that wanted her dead, but it didn't make sense that they would come after Tiffany. She looked around and spotted a fountain in the corner of the yard. Tiffany stood up with her tea and walked towards the fountain. She loved the peacefulness of the water sound. She kneeled and ran her hands through the water. Tiffany jumped when she heard a branch break in the distance. She stood up and looked in the direction she heard the noise. She had a cold chill run up her spine, but she shrugged it away. All she saw was trees moving from the wind and birds eating off the ground.

Tiffany turned and walked around to the opposite side of the fountain where the water ran into a pond. She saw a few lily pads and flowers blooming from the pond. She was surprised anything would grow in the chilly weather. Tiffany slid her hands in her pocket and looked back to the woods. She couldn't shake the feeling that someone was watching her. She forced her mind to think it was an animal and she looked back down at the pond. She missed her home and her job. She even missed her sister and wished things had been different between them. Tiffany felt a tear run down her cheek, but didn't even bother to wipe it away.

***

Briggs and Michael had been working in the office for what felt like hours. They were no closer to finding who was framing Tiffany then they were on day one. Briggs felt a headache coming on and rubbed the back of his neck. He walked over to the window and pulled back the curtains. He didn't plan on seeing Tiffany in the yard. He shut the curtain and walked out of the office to the front door. He opened the door as quiet as he could and hoped Tiffany didn't hear him. To his surprise she didn't and he shut the door behind him. He walked over to the post where the steps started and leaned up against a post. He felt like he could watch her all day.

Briggs looked at her hair first; it was down and had a slight wave to it. He loved how it passed her shoulders and framed her face. He looked at her body and wondered how everything she wore fit her so perfect. She was wearing a gray sweater and a black scarf around her neck. She had on tight blue jeans and some black boots that her jeans were tucked into. He admired her curves that still showed under the sweater. Yes he was attracted to Tiffany, but surprisingly he was more attracted to her personality. She was a kind person with so many amazing thoughts.

Tiffany intrigued Briggs. He wanted to know more about her and felt like it was never enough when she would talk. He watched Tiffany look down at the pond and he felt a part of his heart break. It wasn't until then that he noticed the tear on her cheek running down her face. She crossed her arms and hugged herself. Briggs felt the need to be near her, but he also felt his heart pull him back. He didn't want to get too close to her. He had to protect her from a killer not a broken heart. He turned and headed to the front door. Guilt washed over him as he walked inside and shut the door. No matter what he told himself, he knew he would never get over the feeling of letting her down.

Briggs walked back into the office and saw Michael sitting at the desk. Once he walked in, Michael turned and looked at Briggs.

"What are you so afraid of Briggs? It's not like she doesn't like you and you don't like her."

Briggs figured Michael must have been watching him out the window. He wasn't mad about it, but he didn't want to talk about it either.

"It's nothing, so let's start back at the beginning again. What are we missing?"

He was hoping Michael would let the Tiffany thing go, but he knew better than that.

"Look, you know I'm not going to stop until you talk to me. You better just get it over with."

Briggs looked down at his feet before he sat down on the couch.

"You're right. I do like her and I think she likes me."

Michael laughed before he said, "I got that part, Briggs. What is the reason you are staying away from her like you're afraid?"

Briggs cleared his throat and felt sweat building in his hands.

"It's not easy to explain. I just don't want to get close to her right now. I need to protect her and I can't do that if my mind is always on her."

Michael's face changed and he got serious.

"You are worried that she will get hurt like Britt almost did?"

Biggs sighed and looked in Michael's eyes.

"That's about right. I just don't want to be distracted with Tiffany and then someone hurt her. I would never forgive myself."

Michael sat back in his chair.

"Briggs, I still beat myself up about how close Brittany came to getting hurt. The thing is, I finally realized that if I never would have fallen in love with her then I never would have fought as hard as I did to keep her alive. I became more protective of her the more I loved her. You can't live your life with the "what-ifs". You have to live with what you are sure of and right now your feelings are pretty dead on. I know that my love for Brittany isn't what almost got her killed, it's what saved her from getting hurt."

Briggs watched Michael walk out of the room. He never looked at things the way Michael had put them. He always thought Michael blamed himself for almost getting Brittany hurt, but really he didn't. Briggs was starting to question everything he thought. Maybe he would give him and Tiffany a chance.

***

Michael heard his phone ring and ran to the kitchen to get it. He looked down at the caller ID and saw it was his chief.

He answered it in a stern voice, "Sims."

Chief Belue cleared his throat and said, "Michael, we have some news. One of the insurance adjusters that were looking at Tiffany's house today had a woman come asking questions about the house. They didn't think anything about it until they realized that Tiffany was being hunted by a killer. They called it in a little while ago and I'm having the guy come in for questioning in the morning. I want you and Briggs here at eight to talk to him. I'm also having the guy sit down with a sketch artist and see what pans out. It could lead up to nothing but I just want to be sure. How are y'all coming along with the case anyway?"

Michael was glad to hear there might be a lead, but he wasn't looking forward to telling Chief Belue that they weren't getting anywhere with the case.

"Well, what you have told us is our first real lead. We have all our phone lines traced in case someone calls, and we have cops outside the house around the clock. We looked into Tiffany's mom, but still haven't found her yet. It looks like she just disappeared off the face of the earth. We are working with the fire department and bomb squad to try to figure out the type of bomb that was set. So far, they don't have any prints on any of the fragments and it looked like it was a sensor bomb. When Briggs opened the door, it set the bomb off."

Michael heard his chief sigh.

"Well, maybe this will help us get somewhere in the case. Stay safe and I'll see y'all in the morning."

With Chief Belue hung up. Michael ran his fingers

through his hair and set his phone on the counter. He didn't understand how someone could be so careful and not leave one clue. He was worried they might just get away with everything.

***

Briggs walked into the kitchen as Michael hung up the phone. He walked to the bar and pulled out a seat. Sitting down, he looked up at Michaels face.

"Was that the boss?"

Michael nodded his head and Briggs heart started beating. He really wanted the news to be good but wondered if it was bad.

"He said the insurance adjuster was at Tiffany's house and someone came up asking questions. The guy got a bad feeling and called it in. He heard that Tiffany was in the middle of a murder and attempted murder investigation so he called. We have a meeting with the guy in the morning and he is also working with a sketch artist. Boss said it could be nothing, but my gut tells me it was the killer asking questions."

Briggs agreed with Michael; something about it told him it was the killer.

"That's great! This could be our first really good lead."

Michael nodded and the front door opened. Tiffany walked in and hung her scarf on a hook. Michael looked at Briggs and winked.

"Well, I'm going to go find Britt. Remember what I said. It might save her."

Michael walked away and Briggs looked over at Tiffany. She walked past him and went to the fridge. She grabbed a soda and sat at the opposite side of the bar.

"Are you any further with the case? I saw y'all in the office working."

Briggs contemplated on whether to tell her about the new lead, but he didn't see her running off telling anyone any time soon.

"We just got a call from Chief about someone asking questions around your house. We are going to talk to someone in the morning about what was said."

He could see the shimmer of hope in her eyes. He didn't want her to get her hopes up so he decided to make sure she knew it could be nothing.

"Tiffany this could be a dead end. We're looking into it, but I don't want you to be upset if it's nothing."

Her face never changed and he was glad it didn't. He watched her walk off towards the living room and he decided to follow her. Michael's words were ringing in his head and he was starting to think more and more that Michael was right.

Briggs sat down on the couch with Tiffany and left a tiny space between them.

"Do you want to watch a movie? Maybe it will take your mind off of everything. We can even watch a chick flick."

Briggs looked over at her and smiled. Tiffany laughed.

"Okay, let's watch a chick flick."

Briggs was happy to hear her laugh. It sent chills over his body and made his stomach get warm. He wished she would do it more often. Tiffany ended up picking out the movie The Time Travelers Wife. He hadn't seen it before, but remembered seeing some previews for it a few years back. He pulled a blanket off the back of the couch. She smiled and took the blanket from him.

Half way through the movie he decided to make his move. He reached his hand over and grabbed hers. She didn't pull away so he pulled her over to him. She leaned over and laid her head on his shoulder and he wrapped his arm around her. With his other hand, he began to run his fingers through her hair. He liked spending time with Tiffany. He only hoped she felt the same way; otherwise he would look like a complete jerk. For now, he just wanted to enjoy the moment in case it didn't happen again.

Briggs watched the rest of the movie holding Tiffany in his arms. He was surprised at how much he liked the movie, but knew he would never admit it. Once the movie went off, Tiffany sat up and looked at him. He felt the need to kiss her but held back. He needed to talk to her about things first.

"Tiffany, I wanted to talk to you about something."

Tiffany's eyes got wider and she had a curious look on her face.

"Protecting you is my number one priority. I will do anything to keep you safe. It's my job to keep you safe, but that's not the only reason I am willing to risk my life for you."

Briggs felt his heart speed up. He never had to explain himself to another woman like this. No other women had given him the chance to talk so this was all new to him. His feelings were on overdrive right then and he was nervous he would mess up.

"Look, what I am trying to say is I have feelings for you and I have kept my distance because I am worried it will get in the way of this case. I don't want my feelings to get you hurt or get me distracted. I am doing the best I can to ignore them, but I don't know how much longer I can put them to the side. What I'm trying to say is, if you're okay with me having feelings for you and you have the same feelings, then we can take this extra slow. I just wanted you to know how I feel and if you don't feel the same way then I'll back off from you."

Tiffany turned to the side and crossed her legs on the couch facing him.

"Briggs, I feel the same way and the only reason I haven't talked to you about it is because I was afraid you didn't feel the same way. I knew how serious this job was to you too. I know what complications it could cause to have feelings for each other. I am happy you talked to me about this because I was driving blind in all this. I'm also willing to take things really slow and just go with the flow of things."

Briggs let out a breath he didn't know he was holding. That was the longest thirty-four seconds of his life. He smiled at her and watched her sit back down on the couch. She cuddled up next to him and laid her head back on his shoulder.

"This time we will watch a dude movie and then we will go to bed. Don't worry, you can sleep with me, but that's all we are doing is sleeping so don't get any ideas there, pretty boy."

Briggs laughed loud and wrapped his arm back around her. He was glad they had cleared things up and could stop hiding their feelings. The next problem was making sure they took things slow and Briggs was worried he wouldn't be able to.

CHAPTER SIXTEEN

Michael woke up to Brittany lying in bed sleeping. He was surprised that she wasn't getting sick in the bathroom like she had been for a week straight. He looked over at his clock on the nightstand and saw it was six-thirty. He decided to get up and get his day started. He rolled out of bed as quiet as he could and headed to the bathroom. He heard Brittany roll over, so he decided to get his clothes and take a shower downstairs so he wouldn't wake her up. He gathered up his clothes, soap, and deodorant. When he got to the bottom of the stairs he found Briggs in the kitchen drinking a cup of coffee. He shook his head and walked to the bathroom. It was too early to talk to anyone and he wasn't a morning person until he had a shower and coffee.

Michael finished with his shower and got dressed. He walked to the kitchen and found Briggs still there drinking coffee. He went to the pot and poured himself a cup and checked the time. It was seven-fifteen and he needed to hurry so he could get to the office. He was a little worried about leaving Brittany and Tiffany alone in the house, but he already made preparation for two additional officers to come in and stay while they were gone. Having three cops standing guard eased his mind. Michael heard a knock at the door and Briggs looked up at him with a questioning look.

"It should be the two cops that'll sit with the girls while we are gone."

Briggs jumped up and headed to the door. Michael thought he heard Briggs say he would get it, but he couldn't be sure. He hadn't finished his coffee and without it his hearing was gone. Michael heard voices and headed to the door. He was shocked to see Mark and Taylor standing in the doorway. He didn't expect them to be at the house, especially not so early in the morning.

"Hey guys, what are y'all doing here so early in the morning?" Taylor walked in behind Mark and Briggs shut the door. Taylor stepped around Mark and spoke.

"We know y'all have a lot going on right now and we wanted to help out. So, we are here for anything y'all need. Plus, we all know how it gets being cooped up in a house all alone."

Taylor smiled and Michael felt a ping of guilt hit him. He refused to think back to those bad memories so he pushed them to the side and flashed Taylor a smile.

"Well, Britt and Tiffany are still asleep. We're heading to the station to get some work done. If y'all want to keep them company that would be great. I have two extra cops coming over to sit on the house while we are gone. I'll just have them sit at the front and back of the house. We shouldn't be gone long, but we aren't sure. Britt will be excited to see y'all here and I'm sure Tiffany will enjoy the company as well."

Taylor walked past Michael and went to the kitchen.

"Okay, well I am going to make them breakfast and don't worry I know Britt has a sensitive stomach right now. I have one too so I won't cook heavy stuff. Go get some work done. We will be here when you get back."

Michael smiled and shook Mark's hand. After Michael said his goodbyes, he and Briggs left for the station.

Michael checked in with his boss at seven forty-five and headed to one of the interrogation rooms. Briggs went to grab the sketch Michael had done from his wreck. Something told him it was the same girl that tried to kill him. Michael sat down with his pen, paper, and recorder. He looked over at the door when it opened and saw Briggs walk in with another guy.

"Michael, this is the insurance adjuster, Austin Plause."

Michael pointed to the seat in front of him and Briggs laid a folder down in front of Michael. Mr. Plause sat down at the desk and looked at Michael with a stern look.

"Mr. Plause, I just want to inform you I am recording this conversation. I am in no way implicating you as a suspect at this time and the questions I am going to ask you are related to information you provided us yesterday. Do you agree with being recorded and not having a lawyer present?"

Mr. Plause looked at Michael, confused at first. "Do I need a lawyer present?"

Michael rolled his eyes because he wished people listened more carefully.

"No, Mr. Plause, you don't need a lawyer. Again, you are not a suspect and we are only questioning you about an incident you reported that might help a current case."

He nodded his head and said he agreed. Michael began with his questions.

"Do you remember what time you went by the house of the victim, Tiffany Childress?"

He looked off in the distance as if to collect his thoughts.

"It was around noon when I got to her house. I know for sure of the time because I left another house two streets over at eleven fifty-five."

Michael jotted some notes down at the time of arrival.

"Did you tell anyone outside of work that you would be visiting Ms. Childress' house?"

He looked down at his hands and Michael worried he would lie. When people looked away and not in his eyes, it usually meant they are lying. Just as Michael began to worry about his credibility, he looked up into Michael's eyes and Michael knew he wouldn't lie.

"No, just my wife. I tell her where I'm going in case she needs to find me. We had a scare a few weeks ago and my phone was dead. She thought she was going into labor and couldn't get a hold of me, since then I always tell her my schedule in case she can't reach me."

Michael nodded his head and jotted more stuff down on the paper.

"Do you know how long you were there before the person in question approached you?"

He looked at Michael in the eyes again.

"I wasn't there long, maybe fifteen minutes."

Michael wrote down that the killer had to be there waiting because Mr. Plause wasn't there long enough before someone approached.

"Do you remember what direction the person came from?"

He looked off in the distance again.

"Now that you mention it she came from beside the house, almost near the bushes. I don't think I really thought about it much because I figured she was a neighbor."

Michael looked at him a little confused.

"Why would you think she was a neighbor because of the direction she came from?"

"Well, it was the questions she asked me. She made it sound like she was concerned about Ms. Childress."

Michael wrote down everything he said.

"Let's back up a little bit. What was the first thing she said when she approached you?"

He looked over at Briggs and back at Michael.

"She walked up and asked if she could talk to me for a second. I said yes and she started talking about how horrible it was that Tiffany was going through everything. She then asked if Tiffany was okay and wanted to know if she needed anything. I told her that as far as I knew she was okay and that I wouldn't really know if she needed anything. I started to walk away so I could get my work done, but she followed me. She asked me if I knew what hotel she was staying at so she could go and check in on her. I told her that I didn't have that kind of information, but she could leave her a letter or note in the mailbox and maybe Ms. Childress would get it. She then asked if I had a number so she could just call instead and I told her that I wasn't allowed to give out any of that information. She smiled at me, but didn't say anything. It was weird. When she finally spoke she told me to let Ms. Childress know that she would leave a note in the mailbox. I walked away and went back to work."

Michael wrote everything down and looked over at Briggs. He had gotten the message Michael was trying to send and walked out of the room.

"So, Mr. Plause, here is a sketch of what we think the girl looks like. Can you look at it and tell me if you think it's her? If it's not her then we can have a sketch artist come in for you."

Michael slid the sketch over to him and waited for him to speak and it didn't take long.

"Yeah that's her! The only thing missing is the tattoo she had on her neck. It was on the right side of her neck and it was some letters. I don't remember what the letters were. Maybe S-A-C or S-A-P?"

Michael stood up and said, "Well, you have been more help then you know. If you think of anything else, please give me a call. Also, I might be calling for a follow up in a few days."

Michael turned the recorder off and slid the sketch back in the folder. He shook Mr. Pause's hand and they both left the room. Michael was hoping the note was still in the mailbox. He was sure his gut was right, and the killer came back to the scene.

***

Brittany woke up and headed downstairs. She smelled food and surprisingly was hungry. She figured Tiffany cooked breakfast because Michael and Briggs were gone to the station. She had a lot to do and forgot to tell Michael about any of it. She made a mental note to call him and let him know about her plans. She needed to go help Tiffany get her sisters stuff and put it in storage and then she needed to go get Tiffany's sisters cat. She got to the bottom of the stairs and found Tiffany sitting at the kitchen table in her pajamas. She heard a familiar laugh and turned to see Taylor and Mark cooking in the kitchen.

Brittany lost control and ran over to Taylor. She hugged her as tight as she could. She was so happy to see them both. She hated being cooped up in the house and seeing their faces was like a breath of fresh air.

"What are you two doing here?"

Taylor stepped back from Brittany and said, "We knew you would get cabin fever so we came for a visit."

Brittany pulled Taylor back in for another hug and laughed.

"I am so sorry I wasn't down here to introduce y'all to Tiffany! If I knew you would be here, then I would have gotten up a long time ago."

Taylor laughed.

"Yeah, we already met, and she tells me y'all have some plans of packing up stuff and picking up a cat. Y'all want some help?"

Brittany looked at Tiffany and waited for her to answer. After all, it was her dead sister's stuff and Brittany worried she wouldn't want many people going through it all.

"We would really love the help as long as y'all don't mind?"

Taylor waved her hand and shoved a pancake in her mouth. Brittany knew she wouldn't mind helping plus it helped having Mark to lift the heavy stuff.

Everyone spent the morning laughing and getting to know Tiffany a lot better. Outside of her shell, she was a very happy and sweet woman. Brittany was glad to see that side of her. Brittany left them all to talk and went to the living room to call Michael. He answered on the first ring as Brittany knew he would.

"Hey, babe. I was calling to let you know that me, Mark, Taylor, and Tiffany are going to move stuff out of Tiffany's sister's house. She has to get it out and she could use the help. We will take two cops with us and leave one here.

Also, we have to go get a cat from the vet's office."

She waited for Michael to tell her no, but he didn't.

"Okay, Britt, but be careful please. Promise you will take two cops and keep an eye out for anything unusually weird."

Brittany finished her conversation with Michael and joined everyone in the kitchen. They put a plan together on the best way to move the stuff to storage. Brittany decided to rent a U-Haul truck. Tiffany called and rented a storage building not far from the apartment. Brittany and Tiffany went to their rooms and got ready so they could go. Brittany was just excited to get out of the house and she really didn't care what it was she was doing.

***

Michael almost ran out of the office to find Briggs outside. He had just gotten off the phone with Brittany and got the okay from his chief to look for the note. He watched Briggs pull around in his truck and Michael jumped in. Michael's heart was racing and he hoped they found the note. He was worried someone got it out of the mail. He looked over at Briggs and saw the look in his eyes. Briggs eyes turned a dark black and his face looked like you could bounce a penny off of it from being so tight. Briggs was on edge more than Michael was and that was rare. Michael held onto the door handle while Briggs sped around a curve.

It didn't take them long to reach Tiffany's house and considering Briggs' speed it made sense why they made it there so fast. Michael jumped out of the truck and Briggs was already at the mailbox. Michael watched Briggs slide on a glove and open the mailbox.

"Briggs, be careful. You don't know what could be in there."

Briggs looked up at Michael and pulled out a stack of

mail. Michael walked over to where Briggs was standing and watching him flip through the mail. Briggs came to an envelope that had Tiffany's first name wrote on the front in red pen. Nothing else was on the envelope so Michael figured it was the note. Briggs slid the other mail under his arm and opened the envelope. Michael waited for Briggs to read the note. Michael slipped on his gloves and reached for the note when Briggs was done with it. Words were written in the middle of the paper in sloppy red ink.

CHAPTER SEVENTEEN

Michael looked at the letter and read it to himself. *You will die and so will everyone you care about. You can't keep hiding. I will find you and I will kill you, bitch. I am always watching you. YOU ARE MINE!*

Michael folded the note before he placed it along with the envelope into an evidence bag. Michael saw the anger in Briggs' face.

"Briggs, calm down and let's think about this. We know it's a woman. We know what she looks like and we also we have information about a tattoo. We are getting closer."

Michael followed Briggs back to the truck.

"Briggs, talk to me!"

Briggs stopped in front of the truck.

"Every day is one day closer to losing Tiffany. This note does nothing but piss me off, and it gets us nowhere. You know as well as I do there won't be one damn print on that paper."

Briggs slammed his fist down on the hood of the truck. Michael couldn't believe it because that truck was Briggs's baby. He never saw Briggs treat it like that so he knew he was pissed.

"Look, you just have to trust me. We will find this bitch and keep Tiffany safe. Let's get back to the station and turn this note into the lab."

Briggs nodded and went to the driver side door. Michael climbed up in the truck hoping that what he said wouldn't come back to bite him in the ass.

***

Tiffany felt weird having Brittany riding in the car with her, but she relaxed a little when they started talking. They kept the conversation light as they talked about music and hobbies. Tiffany kept an eye on the rear-view mirror. Mark and Taylor were right behind them and the cops followed in a squad car. They'd picked up the U-Haul and were heading to Jennifer's house. Tiffany didn't look forward to going through Jennifer's stuff, but she didn't really have a choice. She wanted to get it over with and throw it all in storage. She would eventually be forced to look through everything, but for now it had a safe place in a storage unit.

Tiffany pulled up to the apartment and parked. She cut the truck off and jumped out. Mark, Taylor, and one of the cops were already out of the car.

The cop walked over to Tiffany and said, "Ms. Childress, I will go ahead of you and check everything out. Once it's clear, y'all can go in."

Tiffany handed him the keys and watched him open the door. All Tiffany could think at that moment was how grateful she was that the place didn't blow up like her house did. A few minutes later the cop came out talking into a radio and shut the door behind him. Tiffany felt something was off and immediately got goose bumps. Tiffany watched as the cop walked over to where she was standing.

"Ms. Childress, you can't go in there right now. Right

now, your sister's house is a crime scene."

Tiffany heard the words but didn't understand. A crime scene? Tiffany hands shook and her stomach turned.

"Who is in there?" Tiffany said softly, barely getting the words out.

"We don't know. We only know it's a man."

"Please tell me it's not Briggs?"

The officer shook his head as he spoke into his radio. Once the static from the other end stopped, he turned his attention back to her.

"It's not any of our officers."

He left her and walk back to his squad car. Tiffany walked to the truck and got her phone out. She dialed Briggs' cell number and waited for him to answer.

"You and Michael need to come to my sister's apartment. We are fine, but you just need to get over here now!"

She hung up before he could say anything. She couldn't deal with a thousand questions when she didn't have any answers to give him.

***

When Briggs hung up the phone with Tiffany, he knew he needed to get her. He pulled both visor mirrors down and flipped two switches on the dash. The sirens and lights came on while he pushed the gas harder.

"We have to get to Tiffany. Something is wrong and she didn't say what it was. She said everyone is fine, but we needed to hurry."

As Briggs stopped talking, Michael's phone rang. He didn't hear much of what Michael said because his focus was on the road. When Michael got off the phone, he set his phone down in his lap.

"It was Chief. There's been a murder in Tiffany's sister's house. The body was a male and it's pretty bad. The crime scene techs are on their way and we'll know more once we're there."

Briggs felt his heart slow down a little. He was glad Tiffany wasn't hurt, but he had a bad feeling whoever was dead inside the apartment was a message to Tiffany.

Briggs saw squad cars and a fire truck when he pulled up to Jennifer's apartment complex. Brittany ran up to Michael.

Briggs yelled over the noise to Brittany, "Where is Tiffany?"

Brittany pointed to the fire engine. He ran over to the truck. Tiffany was sitting in the back with an oxygen mask on her face. He ran to her as she dropped her mask and wrapped her arms around his neck. He pulled her close to him and kissed her cheek.

"Are you okay?"

He pushed her away from him and looked into her eyes.

"Yeah, I'm okay. I just had a really bad panic attack."

Briggs pulled her back in for another hug.

"I have to go check out what's going on. Stay here and I'll come back as soon as I can, okay?"

She nodded her head and he headed to towards the apartment.

***

After speaking to Brittany, Michael set out on his way to find a crime scene tech. When he got to the apartment there was a guy at the door with a sign in sheet.

"I'm not going in yet, but can you page the lead crime scene tech to come out for a second please?" Michael said as the guy attempted to hand him a clip board.

The guy nodded and radioed in for someone to come outside. Michael took out a pen and paper, hoping to get some kind of information on what was going on. The tech walked out the door in a white hazmat suit. He waved for Michael to come to the door. Michael walked to the door, but kept his distance.

"Do you at least have a name of the victim and cause of death from the Medical Examiner?"

"Look, I'm going to tell you this the best way I can. This shit is the worst I've seen in twenty-five years. We have no way of identifying who it is yet. We have to gather all the body parts and get them to the lab first. The only thing I can tell you is that it's a man and his death wasn't pretty."

Michael nodded as the tech slipped his mask on and walked back into the house. Michael looked over at the other guy at the door.

"When you get a chance, find out how long they'll be. If it's going to be a while then we might just come back. I'll be over at the squad cars so let me know."

The guy nodded and Michael set off to find Briggs. Michael saw Briggs walking towards him.

He waited until he got close enough to him and asked, "Is Tiffany okay?"

"Yeah, she's okay. A bit shaken, but okay. What did you find out?"

"Not much. They said it's pretty bad and they can't get anything solid about who it is yet. They had to collect body parts before they could identify him. Does Tiffany know who it might be?"

"I don't know. I didn't ask her. I'll talk to her when I get a chance. Did they say how long it would take? I want to get Tiffany home and not make her wait out here forever."

"No," Michael said as he started back to the guy at the door.

The guy already knew what he wanted. He didn't give Michael a chance to say anything before he said, "It will be at least a few hours. They said for y'all to leave and come back. If you want to leave your numbers I'll pass them along and have someone call when they are finishing up."

Michael nodded his head and handed the guy his card. Michael caught up to Briggs and told him to get the girls ready to go. He was ready to get them home and return to the scene. Plus, they had a note to turn into evidence. Michael was hoping the killer had made a mistake in Jennifer's house. He wasn't counting on it, but he could at least hope.

CHAPTER EIGHTEEN

Briggs stopped by the station to drop the note off to the lab before heading back to Michael and Brittany's house. Briggs pulled up in the driveway and waited while Michael went in and checked out the house. Once Michael gave them the okay, everyone got out and went inside. It was only lunch time, but Briggs could tell Tiffany was worn out; she looked pale. Briggs hurt for her and his anger grew every time he looked at her. He wanted everything to be over for her. Tiffany was in bad shape and whoever the bitch was causing the mess, was really getting out of control. He grabbed her hand and walked her to their room. Tiffany sat on the bed and sighed.

"I'll be right back," Briggs told her as he got up.

Briggs found everyone else in the kitchen.

"How is Tiffany doing?" Michael asked.

"Not so good. Brittany do you think it would be okay if Tiffany took a hot bath in your tub? The other tub is small and I want her to try to relax a little."

Brittany looked up at him and smiled.

"Sure, I'll even go start it and put in some bubbles. I have some candles too. I'll light them for her."

Briggs smiled and thanked her. He walked back into the bedroom and found Tiffany on the floor in a corner rocking.

Tears rolled down her face, but not one sob was coming out. She was quiet and starred out into space. Briggs leaned down and picked her up in his arms. She laid her head on his shoulder as Briggs carried her out of the room in his arms. As he walked by everyone in the kitchen, no one said a word. He walked up the stairs and heard water running. He had never been upstairs, so he followed the sound of the water. Briggs went to the first door he saw and found a bedroom; and the sound of water got louder. He stopped and waited for Brittany to come out of the other door. He heard her whisper that a towel and wash rag was sitting out for her.

He whispered to Tiffany, "Do you think you can stand for just a second?"

Tiffany nodded and Briggs set her down.

"I'm going to help you take off your clothes, so don't be alarmed."

She nodded again and with her help Briggs successfully undressed Tiffany. She was cold to the touch and her eyes were glazed over; his heart broke for Tiffany. He picked her up, took a few steps, and placed her in the tub. She didn't even flinch getting into the hot water. Briggs was worried about leaving her alone. Briggs sat down on the floor and put his back up against the cabinets. He looked over at Tiffany and she was staring at him. He smiled at her, but her face stayed blank.

"Please get in with me," she squeaked before looking away.

Briggs stood up and undressed. He stepped into the hot, steamy water and slowly sat down. Brittany poured a ton of bubbles in the water because the bubbles fell over the side of the tub. The water felt good on his body. He felt his way through the water and found Tiffany's feet. He pulled one of them up and out of the water. Slowly and easy he began to massage it. Tiffany's body slid further down in the water as her head rested on the back of the tub. He was glad to see her relax a little and was willing to do anything to help her with it. He tried to fight the feelings that were growing towards her, but he was falling for her hard and there was nothing he could do to stop it.

***

Michael walked onto the back porch where everyone else was sitting. He pulled out a seat at the table and listened to everyone talking. They were all talking about the babies and Michael was glad to have something good to look forward to. Becoming a dad was the main thing that kept his mind off everything that was going on.

Michael felt his phone vibrate on his hip. He pulled it out to see who it was. He didn't recognize the number, but he answered it anyway.

"Detective Sims."

At first no one said anything.

"Sims, this is William Blake. We are finishing up down here, but I want you to come by before we move the body parts. You might see something we didn't and with everything a mess like it is, we could really use another set of eyes."

Michael stood up and walked to the railing of the porch.

"My partner and I will be there ASAP."

He hung up the phone and walked back to the table.

"We have to go back to the scene. Will y'all keep an eye on Tiffany, please? Try to keep her mind off it."

Everyone nodded and Michael walked back into the house. He heard footsteps coming down the stairs and saw Briggs reach the bottom with Tiffany wrapped up in his arms. He gave Briggs a look and Briggs nodded his head. After being partners for a few years, you learn to read a person. Briggs walked back out of the room a few minutes later.

"She is going to lie down and try to get some sleep. What's going on?"

Michael motioned for Briggs to follow him outside.

Once they got outside Michael turned, faced Briggs, and said, "The techs want us to come by before they move the body. Everyone is going to look out for Tiffany while we're gone. We need to get moving while everything is still there."

Briggs nodded and walked back towards the door. Before he opened the door, he turned to Michael.

"Give me five minutes. I'll meet you at the truck."

Michael nodded and hopped in the truck. It wasn't long before Briggs climbed into the truck. The ride to the apartments was quiet. Michael was worried about Briggs, but they had more important things to worry about; a chopped up dead body in a murdered girl's apartment.

***

Briggs pulled up to the apartment. The scene wasn't the same as it was a few hours before. There were no fire trucks and the majority of the squad cars were gone. He was ready to get to work, but he also worried about what was hiding behind the doors. He parked the truck and jumped out with Michael not far behind him. Briggs took the sign-in sheet from the guy at the door and passed it to Michael. The guy handed them some booties and gloves. He and Michael slid on the booties and gloves then entered the apartment.

The lead tech walked to the door to meet them both.

"Hello gentlemen. You know the drill. Be sure to watch where you step and let us know if we need to photograph anything. We have everything marked and ready to go into evidence bags. First, we start at the door. Someone broke in and it looks like they used a crowbar or maybe a sharp tool. Either way the door frame is badly damaged."

Briggs saw the frame pulled apart from the door. He looked past the tech and saw something that turned his stomach upside down.

"As you can see, here is where it gets messy. The murderer used a nylon rope to hang the head of the victim from the ceiling by the hair. We aren't sure of the tool they used yet, but it was a jagged cut almost like they hesitated."

Briggs took a few steps towards the head to examine it. The victim's mouth and eyes were wide open. There were no marks on his face but there was a cut in the middle of his throat.

"We have a good idea where they did it, but we will get to that in a second. We found a note in his mouth. The other techs have it in a bag for you to look at. I will have one of them give it to you once we are done; now onto the living room. This room isn't as bad as the others, but it's still not empty. The murderer cut off the victim's left leg and right arm. They placed the leg on the couch and rammed the arm into the TV."

Briggs looked on the floor and saw glass from the TV and dirt from a potted plant turned over. He looked at the victim's leg on the couch. It had a purple mark around the ankle. He guessed the murderer tied the victim up and the marks were from the restraints. No other marks were visible on the leg, so he moved to the arm. The arm was jammed into the broken TV and sticking out with the hand folded up like it was holding something. He reached for the hand and pried it open.

"There was also a note found inside of the hand. We have it in a bag and will give you that one too. It took a lot of force to ram an arm into a TV and make it stay."

Briggs looked up at the wall and saw some pictures broken and hanging sideways on the wall. *Whoever did this was angry beyond words.* The tech walked past them and into the kitchen.

"In here we found the other arm in the oven and the other leg on the counter. The hand also had a note in it. We have it in a bag and will give it to you with the others."

Briggs' mind was going crazy. The murderer must have left some evidence in the mess. There just didn't seem to be anyway you could do that much damage and not leave a bread crumb. He bent down and looked at the arm in the oven. There was a cut on the arm near the wrist that looked like a scratch.

"Did y'all get a swab of the scratch on the arm?"

The tech nodded.

Briggs looked at the leg on the counter and noticed the same marks as the other leg had. The kitchen didn't look as much of a mess as the living room. Nothing seemed to be moved out of place.

The tech turned and walked towards a hallway near the living room. There were three doors and Briggs watched him open the first door on the right.

"We didn't find a body part in here, but we did find a note hanging from the ceiling by a rope. They've got it in a bag."

The deeper they got into this house the more Briggs wished it was over. He had never seen anything like it in his life. He didn't know how much more his stomach could take. The smell was horrible and the sight of the body parts was getting to be a lot. They left the laundry room and walked to another door down the hall. The tech opened the door and Briggs almost lost his stomach.

"This room shows how messed up in the head our murderer is. From the blood to the body parts it took us the most time to process this room. We don't believe the murderer cut him up in this room."

Briggs looked around and saw bloody hand prints on the walls but no blood on the floors. On the bed was the victim's torso but his penis was cut off and hanging by a rope on the ceiling. The dresser drawers were pulled out and all the clothes were thrown on the floor. Briggs looked at Michael and noticed his face was white. Briggs knew Michael was close to losing his stomach too.

"We'll keep moving but you should know there was another note in here too. It was nailed to the torso. Again, we have it bagged."

Briggs was curious as to what the notes said, but he was also ready to get out of the house. The tech walked out of the room past them and opened a door that was further down the hallway. He stood back and let them look inside.

"This is where we think the murderer cut up the body."

Briggs could see and smell why. The amount of blood in the bathroom was more than he could have ever imagined. The tub looked as if it had been flooded with nothing but blood. The floor had shoe prints on it and the sink was covered with bloody hand prints. In the tub hanging from the ceiling were two ropes with blood on them. The walls surrounding the tub were drenched in blood.

"We think the victim was hanging from the ropes and the murderer cut him up in the tub. The medical examiner thinks he was alive for most of the cutting and likely died from blood loss. He won't know more until we collect all the parts and take them in. Find this son of a bitch and get them off the streets, boys, because I don't want to clean up another one of these again."

Briggs took one last look and walked to the front door. The tech followed.

"We will have the pictures sent to your office and all the evidence sent to the lab. Tomorrow you can come back and search through the house to see what else you can find."

Briggs only nodded, because no words were coming to his mind after everything he had seen. He walked out of the apartment and headed for one of the techs next to a truck. He wanted to see the notes and get home to Tiffany. He needed to figure out how to explain everything because she would be asking questions.

CHAPTER NINETEEN

B riggs waited for the techs to pull out the evidence bags that held all the notes. His heart raced and his palms were sweating. The worst part was his mind couldn't stop seeing all the body parts placed all over the apartment. His stomach turned at the thought of it all. The techs laid all the notes out in order on the tail gate of their truck. Each bag was labeled with where the note was found.

The first note found in the mouth of the victim read; *He was a horrible person that needed to die!*

Briggs had a funny feeling that Tiffany knew the victim and it was going to hurt her. He only hoped it gave them a clue of who could be after her. He looked to the next note and saw it was the note that came from the arm that had been rammed into the TV.

In all capital letters, it read; *YOU ARE MINE!*

Briggs was tired of seeing that message. He couldn't get those three words out of his mind. Why did the killer keep saying that? How was Tiffany theirs? It just didn't make any sense to him. Especially, if the only suspect they had was a woman.

The next note was found with the arm that was in the oven. It was also in red ink on the paper and read; *I will come back for you!*

Briggs wondered if that meant the killer was going to hide out for a while. He was worried that Tiffany might be looking over her shoulder for a long time. Then again, he could be wrong and the killer was just trying to throw them off and let their guard down. He would never leave Tiffany alone until that bastard was caught.

The next note that was hung by a rope in the laundry room was also written in red ink and it read; *They can't protect you forever!*

Briggs was already angry but seeing that note made his blood pressure rise even more. The killer might think he couldn't protect Tiffany forever, but he was betting his life that he would.

The last note was found on the torso of the victim nailed to his chest read; *Only I can set you free!*

That was the most confusing note out of them all. Briggs didn't understand why Tiffany needed to be set free. What did she need to be set free from? Was Tiffany hiding something from her past and not telling him? None of the notes added up to him. The crazy fuck acted as if they were doing Tiffany a favor by trying to kill her. His mind was racing and his head started to throb. He knew he would end up with a migraine if he didn't slow it down. He took out his phone and snapped a picture of each note. Then he looked up at the techs and nodded to both of them before heading to his truck.

Michael was silent most of the ride to his house. Briggs could tell he was thinking just as hard as he was, but nothing was making sense to him either. Briggs finally turned into the driveway and parked his truck.

"I don't want to give Tiffany too many details, but I can't keep her in the dark either. Let's just gather everyone together at one time and put our heads together. We'll leave out the blood and gory details. If she pushes the subject of details, I won't keep her from it; after all she does deserve to know what we found. We have to find this mother fucker before they hurt Tiffany."

Michael nodded and got out of the truck. Briggs followed behind him to the front door. Once the door opened Briggs noticed that everyone was staring at him and Michael from the living room. Tiffany was on the couch wrapped in a blanket and Brittany was sitting close to her. Michael sat down in a recliner in the corner and Briggs took the other recliner in the other corner. He sat back and let out a deep breath he didn't notice he was holding in. Tiffany shifted so she could see him better. Taylor and Mark turned around to face him too. He fought to find the words of where to even start. Briggs stood up because sitting down made him more nervous.

"I won't go into details, but I will tell you the body they found was a male. We won't have an ID on the guy until they get him back to the coroner's office. For now, we have evidence to go through. I'm not going to lie to you. It was the worst crime scene I have ever seen. It will take some time to get all the evidence together and back from the lab. Right now, our first lead is the notes that were left at Jennifer's house. I took pictures of them all and I'm hoping you can make some sense of them Tiffany. Don't stress yourself out if you can't put it all together tonight. I don't want you more upset then you already are."

Tiffany was pale, and Briggs could see her hands shaking.

"I'll look at them and see what I can do to help. I want this all over with and if my helping will do that then I'm all in."

Briggs nodded and led her to their room. He wanted to be alone with her for a little while just to keep her calm. He worried if she was in a room full of people then she wouldn't be able to focus. Briggs shut the door behind them when they reached the room. Tiffany walked over to the bed and sat down.

"Take your time and listen to me. I am going to have to give you some details of what we found and I want you calm."

Tiffany nodded her head and took in a deep breath. Briggs pulled out his phone and looked over at Tiffany. Her eyes were big and he knew her heart was beating fast.

"First, let me say when everything is out of the apartment and the cleaning crew comes in, I won't let you go in and get anything out. Michael and I will go in and get the important stuff. The apartment was a mess and I would rather you didn't go inside it again."

Tiffany's face changed.

"I know it might have been bad, but I have to go in and get all my sister's stuff out. I can't and won't leave anything."

Briggs decided to let that argument go for the time being. He could always bring it up later.

"Okay, but back on track. Tiffany, we found five notes in different areas of the house. The first note we found was this one."

Briggs opened his phone and showed Tiffany the picture. She mouthed the words as she read them. She looked at him confused.

"I don't know who it was so I can't really help with that one yet."

Briggs nodded and slid the picture over to the "You are

mine" note. Briggs saw Tiffany's hands start to shake.

"Take a breath, Tiffany."

She looked up at him.

"Why does it seem like they are obsessed with me? I get the feeling they don't want anyone else to be near me. I don't understand."

Tears started to fall from Tiffany's eyes. Briggs wondered if showing her the notes was a good idea. He put his phone down and held her in his arms. She didn't cry long. She pushed him away and wiped her eyes.

"Show me the next one. I need to do this."

"Are you sure?" Briggs asked as he picked up his phone and slid the screen to the "I will come back for you" picture.

Tiffany looked back up to him and said, "I don't understand. Are they going to leave me alone for a while and then come back to kill me? I can't live my life here in this house forever!"

"We won't let that happen, Tiffany. We will find who did this. "

Tiffany nodded and looked down at his phone. He slid his finger over the phone again to the "They can't protect you forever" picture. Tiffany looked up at him and he slid the phone to the last picture. Tiffany didn't say anything and Briggs was about to speak when she finally spoke.

"They have to be obsessed with me. That's the only thing I can come up with. I just don't get why or who would be that obsessed with me."

Briggs thought for a second about what she was saying. She was right about one thing. Whoever was after her; was only doing it because they were obsessed with her.

"Stop for a second and think. Who do you know that might have been obsessed with you? Think back even to your childhood Tiffany; it could be that far back."

Tiffany looked off towards the wall.

"I don't know anyone. Jennifer and I didn't have friends growing up because we were in so many foster homes. Then once we were out and on our own the only person we both knew was my fiancé. I don't have friends and even at work I don't talk to anyone. I keep to myself and always have."

Briggs had a feeling he knew who the dead body was in Jennifer's apartment, but he wouldn't say anything to Tiffany yet.

"Why don't you lie down and try to relax? I have to go talk to Michael and see if he has come up with anything."

Tiffany nodded her head and laid on the bed. Briggs leaned over and kissed her forehead. He walked out of the room closing the door behind him. Everyone was gone from the living room. No one was in the kitchen, but he saw Mark standing on the back deck. He figured everyone was outside. He opened the door and walked out to talk to everyone. He hoped someone had come up with something because he was ready for a solid lead.

Briggs walked over to Michael and everyone joined in around them.

"I think I know who the body was in the apartment, but I don't want to tell Tiffany just yet."

No one spoke, anticipating his words.

"I think it's Tiffany's ex-fiancé. It hit me when I was reading the notes to Tiffany over. That's the only person it could be because Tiffany wasn't close to anyone else but him. Plus, it's the only thing that connects Tiffany to her sister. Jennifer slept with him and that's what made Tiffany leave him."

Briggs waited for someone to speak. Mark was the first to speak up.

"It sounds like whoever is after Tiffany wants to eliminate anyone who has ever had anything to do with her. I hate to say it, but I don't think they will stop until they have her."

Briggs knew Mark was right but he didn't want to believe it. Michael walked to the steps on the porch and Briggs went to join him.

"Tell me what you're thinking, Mike."

Michael looked over to Briggs and said, "I don't think we will find much if any evidence in that house. It was a mess in there, but I don't think they are that stupid to make a mistake that big. I have a bad feeling they are going quiet for a while. Something about that note saying they would be back is really bothering me."

"They're waiting on us to let our guard down, because we can't protect her forever."

Michael only nodded his head. Briggs knew he would have to wait on the evidence to come back. He just prayed the bastard made a mistake.

CHAPTER TWENTY

A week had passed since Michael and Briggs found the body in Jennifer's apartment. The evidence was finally back and Michael was riding with Briggs to the office to get word on what was found. Briggs pulled his truck up and parked in the lab parking lot. He was wound up tight and he just wanted something to come up to give them a lead. He knew Michael wanted it too, but he also knew Michael didn't think there would be much. Briggs reached the door first and held it open for Michael. They walked in and found the same lab tech they'd spoke to when about Jennifer's stabbing.

"Well, I can't say it's good to see you both again on these terms. I don't even know where to start. We ended up with a lot of finger prints, but only one set didn't have a match. The first match we found was on one of the notes. The one listed hanging in the laundry room. It came back as a Tiffany Childress."

Briggs heart stopped. How in the hell was Tiffany's prints on that paper?

"I looked into the prints a little more and found that they were planted like the others. I also took prints from the hands y'all found and it came back as a Justin Wilder. Then we had another set of prints in blood on the wall in the bedroom. Those are the prints that didn't come back with a match. I filed them so y'all could see for yourself. The next thing we move to is the rope. It's nothing special. You can find it at just about any hardware store. The ropes in the bathroom had some DNA on them, but it was linked back to Justin Wilder. The marks on the legs matched the ropes. My guess is that he was hung by his feet while the murder cut him up. He didn't have any defensive wounds on his hands so he didn't fight back. His toxic screen came back with Propofol; a heavy drug that most anesthesiologist use for their patients. There wasn't much in his system so he was more than likely awake to feel the murderer cut him up. I looked at every cut on the body parts and my guess is a hand saw was used. I believe this because of the roughness of the cuts and because there was saw dust in some of the cuts. I also noticed a high amount of testosterone in his system. My guess is he was aroused not long before he was drugged and cut up."

Briggs was writing everything down and trying to keep up.

"Nothing else was out of the ordinary except for the shoe print. The print was small so it either has to be a small man or a woman. Did y'all have any questions for me?"

Briggs looked to Michael hoping he had some questions because he was clueless at what to ask. Michael finally said something.

"Did they find any hair or fibers at the scene?"

The tech looked down at his paperwork.

"I almost forgot about that. They did find some hair, but there wasn't any DNA on it, so the test came back with nothing. As for fibers, there wasn't any. I know it's hard to wrap your head around how someone could make a mess so big, but not leave one bread crumb. I can only say they were careful."

Before Briggs knew what he was doing, he slammed his

fist down on the table. He wanted answers and that was his only chance to get them. He walked out leaving Michael to talk to the tech. He knew there wasn't anything else he needed to hear so he went to the truck to wait on Michael.

Michael jumped up in the truck and Briggs drove out of the parking lot and headed to their office. Briggs was confused and didn't know where to turn.

"What do we do now, Mike?"

"We have to keep our heads up and keep looking at the evidence. Something has to turn our way, Briggs. We need to let Tiffany know it was her ex that was killed and we need to sit and think everything through. If the killer has left and is waiting to come back, then we will just have to live our lives on the edge. They will make a mistake and when they do we will get them."

Briggs knew Michael was right, but he just hoped that mistake didn't cost someone he cared about their life.

Six months later...

Tiffany and Briggs were on their way to see the progress being made on her house. There was a lot more damage then what they first thought. The past few months were hard for Tiffany. She took a leave of absence from her job, while she battled with depression and anxiety. Luckily, she had Briggs to help her with it. They had come a long way since then and even got closer over time. She never stopped looking over her shoulder. She was grateful that Briggs stayed by her side and hadn't let his guard down. Once they moved out of Brittany and Michael's house she moved in with Briggs. She knew it would be a while before her house was finished, but she knew when it was done, Briggs still wouldn't ever leave her side.

Tiffany was grateful to have Briggs and her sister's cat

in her life. She loved the idea of having a pet, but Briggs not so much. He wasn't an animal lover and he definitely was not a cat lover. She just hoped in time he learned to at least like the cat.

Tiffany and Briggs never talked about their feelings, but she knew how he felt every time they made love. It took two months for Briggs to even make a move on her, but when he finally did there wasn't a day that went by that he didn't show her how he felt. She was in love with Briggs and she knew he was in love with her. They were both too afraid to admit it. Tiffany almost did when they had their first argument. Briggs was upset about her wanting to take a trip away for a weekend. She wanted to get out of town for a little while for a much needed break, but Briggs refused to let that happen. He put up a fight with her every time she brought it up. She finally let it go when he told her about Michael and Brittany going away for a week and a murderer almost killing Mark and Taylor. She was ready for everything to finally be over with.

There wasn't a day that went by that she wasn't looking over her shoulder. Nightmares had taken over her sleep and shadows in the dark had her jumping. Every noise made her scared and she found herself looking inside cars driving by. Tiffany felt herself coming unglued and went and saw a psychiatrist for help. She said it was normal for Tiffany to act that way and it would probably be like that until the killer was caught. She was given sleeping pills, but Tiffany couldn't bring herself to take them. She was too afraid she wouldn't wake up if something went wrong during the night. For the most part things were quiet, but she knew she wouldn't ever be able to be normal.

Briggs pulled up to her house and snapped her out of her memories. She waited in the truck for Briggs to walk around and open her door. It was a routine she'd grown to enjoy. Tiffany jumped out of the truck and looked around at all the cars. She even caught Briggs doing the same thing. Once she felt like no one was watching them, she walked with Briggs to the front door. Everything on the outside looked like a normal house.

She opened the door and saw people all around working. They'd put in new sheetrock and the painters were painting. The floors still had to be done, but in a few weeks someone would be there doing them. She had been debating for a while whether she would sell the house once it was done or keep it. She wanted to sell it because it was just another thing that was keeping the bad memories alive. On the other hand, she didn't want to sell it because it was her first home and she loved it. She still had time to think about it so she pushed the thought aside. Briggs walked over to one of the workers and Tiffany followed.

"How many more weeks do y'all think it will take?"

The guy looked at some paperwork and said, "From what I can tell it will only take two more weeks and you will be good to move back in."

Briggs nodded and Tiffany looked away. She had no idea it would be so soon. She thought it would be another month. She was wrong; she didn't have much time to decide on whether to sell it or not.

Briggs looked over at her and asked, "Are you ready to leave?"

Tiffany nodded and smiled when Briggs took her hand. They walked back to the truck where he opened the door for her again. Once she was inside, it only took a few seconds before he was in the driver seat next to her. The pulled off and drove towards town.

"Do you wanna grab a bite to eat in town?"

She smiled at him and said, "Sure, can we try that new

restaurant?"

Briggs nodded and grabbed her hand. He brought it up to his mouth and kissed it.

***

Michael pulled up to the OBGYN office and walked around to Brittany's door. He opened the door and Brittany got out. She was showing more in her pregnancy and Michael loved it. He was glad they told everyone when they did because in no time Brittany started to show. Her dad took it better then Michael guessed he would. It turned out that he wanted a grandchild. Michael and Brittany were getting their first ultrasound that day. They were scheduled to have one two months prior but the machine was broken and another one had to be ordered. Michael was excited because they were going to find out the gender of their baby. Brittany finally got over being sick all the time, but she took up a new habit which was eating all the time. They made it into the room and waited for the doctor to come in.

"Mr. and Mrs. Sims, it's good to see y'all again. Today we have you scheduled for an ultrasound and to find out the gender of the baby, correct?"

They both nodded their head but didn't speak. Nerves were taking over for them both. Brittany wanted the baby to be a girl and Michael was on her side with it. He, of course, wanted a boy but he loved the thought of a little girl looking just like Brittany.

"The tech will be in here in a moment with the machine. Brittany, can you lay down on the table and roll up your shirt, so I can measure you?"

Brittany nodded and laid back on the table. The doctor took a measuring tape out and measured her stomach. "Your belly is measuring much bigger than you last visit. Has your appetite increased lately?"

Brittany looked shocked but Michael knew the answer to that question.

"Yes I have, but I'm always so hungry. It's like I can't ever get full."

The doctor nodded her head and before she could speak a knock came from the door.

"That must be the ultrasound technician. We will talk more once she is done, okay?"

Michael and Brittany both nodded. The doctor opened the door and left the room. An older lady came in wheeling a machine.

"My name is Dorothy and I'll be doing your ultrasound. The main goal here is to get all the measurements we need of the baby first like heart, kidneys, spine, etc. Then we will try to determine the sex of the baby, okay?"

Brittany nodded as Michael stood up to see what was going on.

"I will print out some pictures of the baby for you to take home and send you home with a disk of them. Feel free to ask questions as we go and don't worry, it doesn't hurt. You are far enough along that we can do an over the belly look at the baby. I will also be able to tell you exactly how far along you are and how big the baby is."

Michael couldn't contain his excitement. He walked over to where Brittany was laying and held her hand. The lady put some cream on the end of a wand and looked at Brittany.

"I warmed the gel so it shouldn't be cold."

She pressed the wand on Brittany's belly and a picture

came up on the screen. Michael felt his stomach drop and his palms getting sweaty. There on the screen was a baby's head. Brittany's grip on his hand got tighter.

"There is your precious baby. Now, I'm going to look around the baby to make sure everything is okay."

She moved the wand all over Brittany's belly but soon stopped. She set the wand down and looked at Michael and Brittany.

"Nothing is wrong, but I do need to get the doctor. Don't panic. I promise nothing is wrong, okay?"

Brittany looked up at Michael then back at the lady. She jumped up and was out the door. Just as soon as she left, she returned with the doctor. She picked up the wand and placed it back on Brittany's belly. The picture of the baby came up. She moved it around and the picture came back up of the baby. Michael was confused about what was going on.

"Mr. and Mrs. Sims, we have good news. You are pregnant with two babies."

Michael heard the words but was lost. Did she just say two babies? Brittany's nails were cutting into Michaels hands.

"Wait, how did we not find this out sooner?"

The doctor looked over to Michael and said, "I am as shocked as you are because all the heart beats I have heard were only one baby. I have seen in very few cases where the second heart beat just isn't loud enough so it doesn't show up. Plus, this is your first ultrasound so we had no way of being sure."

Michael froze as his thoughts were going crazy. He was just getting used to the fact of having one baby and now he had to get used to the fact that he was having two. He didn't want to have another baby for a while, but he didn't have much of a choice.

Brittany's voice brought him out of his trance.

"Michael, it will be okay."

He nodded his head and watched the screen. The doctor walked out and Dorothy kept going with the ultrasound.

"For now, we will call them Baby A and Baby B. Baby A has good kidney function and the heart rate is really good. It's a little hard for me to measure the spine, but I got it. Let's look at Baby B."

She moved the wand around Brittany's belly until the other baby appeared.

"The kidneys look really good and the heart rate is really good on this baby too. The spine looks great as well."

Michael was happy to hear everything was going good.

"Would you both like to know what gender each baby is or do you want it to be a surprise?"

Michael looked over at Brittany and she nodded to him.

"We would like to know what they both are."

Dorothy nodded and moved the wand down Brittany's belly.

"Well Baby B is a boy! Now let's look at Baby A and see what it is."

She moved the wand around again and the picture came clear of the baby.

"Baby A is a girl! You have one boy and one girl; fraternal healthy twins. I would say by the way you are measuring that your about twenty-eight weeks pregnant. Congratulations to you both."

Michael still couldn't get over the fact that he was going to have two babies; a little boy and a little girl. He looked over at Brittany and saw her smile. Michael felt all his nerves and worries wash away. Dorothy wiped off Brittany's belly and rolled the machine out of the room. He kissed Brittany on the head and they waited for the doctor to come back in the room.

CHAPTER TWENTY-ONE

Tiffany was full from her lunch with Briggs. She looked over at him driving and smiled. She loved the look on his face when he was in deep thought. He had a way about him that she just couldn't figure out. No matter how hard she tried she could never know what he was thinking. She loved how mysterious he was, but she sometimes wondered what he really thought about her. She looked away once he turned and spotted her looking at him.

He turned and pulled into the driveway and she unbuckled her seat belt. She saw the house come into view and smiled again. She loved his house because of how simple it was. It wasn't fit for just anyone because it was just right for him. It had a country, rough, and edgy feeling to it just like him. He parked the truck and got out. Before she could reach for the handle, he opened her door. She jumped out and followed him to the door. At the door he put his arm out and she ran into it.

Tiffany stopped and didn't move. Her heart started to beat faster and the hairs on her neck stood up. She didn't want to look over his shoulder, but she finally found the urge to do it. She stood up on her tippy toes to see what he was seeing. On his porch, there was a bright pink gift bag and a purple bow. The front door was open and one of the windows was broken. She didn't notice that Briggs had his gun out. He turned and looked at her and her blood went cold.

"Tiffany, we are going to back up and get into the truck. I need you to stay calm and do everything I say to do."

She only nodded her head because words weren't coming out. He grabbed her hand and pulled her with him to the truck. He pointed his gun in every direction and looked into the woods. She was shaking and scared. Once they got to the truck, he opened the door and she jumped in. He walked to the driver side and got into the truck. She watched him work quickly with his hand and eyes. He grabbed his phone and was talking to someone.

"Get to my house now! Bring the boss and some back up. No, we are fine, but I don't want to enter the house until I have backup."

He hung up the phone and looked at her.

"Get down on the floor of the truck, Tiffany. I don't want anyone to see you if someone is here."

She did as he asked and curled up on the floor of the truck. She watched him look around each window. It felt like hours had passed before anyone showed up. She never heard sirens, but she did hear Briggs' voice change. He sounded almost relieved and she knew someone had come to help. "Tiffany get up in the seat and when I get out I want you to run to the patrol car behind the truck and get in with my chief. Me and Michael are going inside the house to make sure no one is in it."

She got up in the seat and looked him in the eyes. He reached for the door handle, but before he opened it he told her he loved her. She was in shock and couldn't move. She heard his door open and rushed to open hers. In a flash, she was gone to the patrol car. When she got in and shut the door she noticed Briggs had already gone into the house. She didn't pray often, but at that moment she was praying he would come back to her. She needed to tell him she loved him too.

***

Briggs went into the house first with Michael not far behind him. Two other officers went around back and entered his house from the back door. Briggs was careful not to touch anything because he was hoping for some prints. He went to the living room, but nothing looked out of place. He yelled "Clear" and then moved to the kitchen; nothing seemed out of place and no one was in there either. He yelled "clear" again and kept moving. He heard someone else yell clear and he knew they were in his den. He moved to his bedroom, but didn't find anyone there either. He yelled "clear" and moved to the bathroom. The room didn't look touched so he yelled "clear" again.

Briggs walked past Michael to the porch. Michael handed him some gloves and he picked up the bag. He pulled the bow off and handed it to Michael. He pulled out the tissue paper and looked inside. There were some fake flowers and a card inside the bag. He carefully pulled out the flowers and handed them to Michael. Briggs pulled out the card and set the bag down. The envelope had Tiffany's name on it. Pictures fell out of the card and there was a note written inside. He was confused by the card because it looked like something a child would get on their birthday. It had a picture of a lion on the front and in big letters it said Happy Birthday. He read the note out loud.

"I hope you missed me because I sure did miss you. I'm back, Bitch and I'm coming for you. It's time to end this once and for all. I will set you free and they won't stop me!"

Briggs looked at the pictures that fell out of the card. One was of a woman and two children. One of the children looked like a smaller and younger version of Tiffany. Another picture was of him and Tiffany kissing in the park. He remembered that day because it was the first time he admitted to himself he loved her. The next picture was of Tiffany sitting on the back porch swing at his house. She was wearing a dress he bought her and smiling. He put the pictures back in the card and handed it to Michael. He had never been so mad before. He knew the killer would come back, but he still hoped they wouldn't.

Briggs walked back to the patrol car where his chief was standing.

"It's all clear, Boss. We found some stuff in a bag, but besides that everything looks okay. One of my windows was broken and the door was open. I'll have to look some more to make sure nothing is missing. We need to call for a lab tech to come out and dust for prints. Also need to get into your trunk for some evidence bags."

Chief Belue popped the lever to the trunk and Briggs walked to the back of the car to grab some bags. Michael was at the back of the car when Briggs shut the trunk. They slipped the items in bags and Briggs took them to the passenger side of the car. Tiffany was looking at him. He opened the door and she jumped out. Before he could say anything she wrapped her arms around his neck. He waited for her to finish and looked her in the eyes. He could see the tears in her eyes about to fall. He hated to see her cry.

"It's okay Tiffany whoever was in the house is gone."

"I love you, too."

He heard her say the words, but he didn't know if he was just hearing things. He forgot he told her he loved her before he jumped out of the car. He kissed her hard on the lips and pulled away from her. Chief Belue was staring at them, but quickly turned away when Briggs looked over at him.

"Tiffany, I need you to look at what was in the bag and

tell me if any of it means anything, okay?"

She nodded and he held up the first bag with the purple flowers in it.

"My mom used to get me and my sister these when we were children. They were our favorite flowers because they were so hard to find in Virginia."

The wheels in his mind started to turn, but he didn't say a word. He held up the next bag with the picture in it of the two children and a woman. Tiffany's hand flew to her mouth.

"That's me, my mom, and my sister Jennifer. I remember when this picture was taken. My mom had it in a frame in her house, but when we were put in foster care I didn't have a chance to get it."

Briggs didn't bother to show her the other pictures and instead he showed her the card. She didn't move and got a confused look on her face.

"I don't get what this sick bastard wants with me! What in the hell do I have that they want so badly?"

Briggs handed the bags to Michael and pulled Tiffany into a hug. She started to sob into his shoulder. He wanted everything to be over and was going to make damn sure Tiffany was safe.

After everyone left and took the evidence with them, Briggs cleaned up the glass. He found a few boards out back near the shed and put them over the window. Briggs was pissed that after six months of a semi normal life they were back to dealing with everything again. He looked over at Tiffany who was wrapped up in a blanket on the couch. He loved her so much and wished he could end everything going on. Something in his gut told him her mother was behind everything. He just didn't know how to tell her that. He walked out the back door and to the shed. He put the hammer back and went back to the house. Once inside, he turned on the alarms and went to join Tiffany on the couch. He had to tell her what he was thinking and see what she said. He pulled her in his arms and kissed her head.

"Want me to start a fire?"

Tiffany smiled up at him and nodded her head. After making a fire, Briggs sat down on the couch and curled up with Tiffany.

"I want to talk to you about everything going on, okay?"

She looked up at him with her eyes wide and hair a mess. He loved it when she wasn't dressed up. Something about a woman with natural beauty did it to him.

"Okay, so what's on your mind?"

He took a deep breath and came back to his original thoughts.

"I think I have an idea of who is behind all of this. I want you to understand I have no strong evidence to tell me if I'm right or wrong, but I am just telling you what my gut says."

She nodded but never said a word. He knew she was hanging on his every word and in that moment, he wished he could take every word he had said back. It was too late and he had to go through with telling her.

"I think it's your mom, babe. I mean think about it. The flowers, pictures, and notes. It all leads to your mom and plus she has disappeared off the face of the planet. Why would she up and leave you and Jennifer? Who else would be doing this?"

Tiffany looked off to the fire and Briggs knew he hit a nerve. He really didn't want to upset her, but he didn't have a choice. He didn't hide anything from Tiffany and he wasn't going to start. He waited for her to look at him. She had tears in her eyes and he instantly felt his heart breaking. He knew he was the cause of the tears, but he couldn't help it. She needed to know where things were going before it ended up being her mother and hurting her worse. His gut was usually never wrong and that time he would almost bet money it was right.

"I'm not upset with you if that's what you're thinking. I was already putting it together in my mind. I guess it took someone else saying it to make it real to me. I was hoping I was wrong, but I really think you are right. It's the only person that comes to mind. Plus, I don't think it was my ex because I honestly think it was his body in Jennifer's apartment. It's the only person that makes sense to be dead that I know. I hated the bastard for cheating on me, but I never wanted him to die. I was always mad at Jennifer for what she did, but I never thought about her dying. I knew in my heart I would one day talk to her again, but just not now. I wasn't over it and didn't know when I would be. I didn't trust many people back then and it hurt for the one person I had in my life to do something like that. I just don't get why my mom would do all this. That's the one thing that doesn't add up. I mean, think about it, she has been out of mine and Jennifer's life for over sixteen years. So why would she all of a sudden come back and do all of this?"

Briggs knew she was right, but he also knew a killer didn't need a big reason. Killers did murder for a reason, but sometimes the reason didn't always make sense. No matter what he was going to find out the reason why it was all happening.

CHAPTER TWENTY-TWO

Michael pulled up to the office and walked in. Briggs called Michael saying he was dropping Tiffany off with Brittany and Taylor. He figured Briggs would be showing up to the office not long after him. He walked to the conference room and sat down at the table. He knew Chief Belue would get news he was there so he decided to wait. He talked to Briggs the night before about everything. Briggs was hung up on the fact that the killer was Tiffany's mother. Michael could understand why Briggs would think it, but something kept pulling at Michael. His gut was telling him it wasn't her mother. Michael was so deep in thought he didn't hear the door open. He jumped when the door slammed shut.

Michael turned and saw Briggs and his chief walk into the room. He turned back to the table and waited for them to get settled.

"Well boys, I've read through all the reports and I have to say this shit is getting out of hand. Do either one you have any suspects?"

Michael knew he was upset about the case still being open. Briggs looked over to Michael and then back to Chief Belue. Michael wanted to just sit and listen to what everyone had to say before he would speak.

"Like I told Michael last night on the phone, all the evidence has me thinking its Tiffany's mother. The pictures are one key factor, the last time Tiffany saw that picture was in her mother's home before they were shipped off to foster care. Then you have the fact that Tiffany's mother is nowhere to be found. Who would hide like that and not want to be found, unless you planned on doing some shady shit? I just don't see how it could be anyone else. Plus, the notes are written like someone is trying to save her from something. The mother could be obsessed with Tiffany. Think about it. She started at nothing and was a no one. Now she has a good job and a nice house. She made something of herself and her mother hates it."

Michael understood why Briggs was pointing the finger at Tiffany's mother, but his gut still told him different. Michael was lost in thought again and Chief Belue saying his name snapped him out of it.

"Michael, I see you over there thinking hard. What's on your mind?"

"I just don't agree with Briggs." He looked at Chief Belue then to Briggs and continued, "Look, I don't think she is hiding, I think she is dead. I think the killer took Tiffany's mother out first then went after Jennifer. Now they are going after Tiffany. The flowers just mean they know Tiffany and her family. The picture could have gotten taken by anyone. I mean what happened to the house? Who got the house after the girls were put in foster care? They could have gotten obsessed with Tiffany and her family then. Then the notes could be someone who just hates Tiffany and wants her to pay for something. Yeah, I know it seems easy to go after the easy target, but it just doesn't feel right. She could have pissed off anyone. Someone getting coffee and she bumped into them or someone had a dog die at her office. Psychotic killers like this one don't need much of a reason to hate someone. Look, all I'm saying is keep your mind open to other things because you could be wrong."

Briggs looked away and Michael knew he was mad at him. Briggs would just have to get over it because Michael wanted their minds in the right direction. Michael looked at his chief who was writing in a notebook. He looked up at Michael.

"I think you both should check out every gut feeling you have. Right now, we have nothing to help us find who this is. Find the damn mother and go from there. I want this case closed!"

He got up and walked out of the room. The door slammed behind him.

Briggs looked over at Michael and said, "I'm telling you it's the mother."

Michael stood up and replied with, "You could be right, but I'm just trying to look in all directions right now. I don't want us searching and end back at square one."

Briggs stood up and followed Michael out of the room.

"You're right. We should look into it better. Look, I'm going to go see if I can't find someone to help me track down Tiffany's mom. Can you look at the evidence again and see what you can come up with?"

Michael nodded and went towards his office. He set down at his desk and pulled up the crime scene pictures. He knew something was there, but he just didn't know where or what it was. He was sure of one thing; he was going to stare at the evidence until what he was looking for slapped him in the face.

***

Tiffany was on edge because of the past events and she could feel her mind slipping. She was worried that the trauma she was being put through would only leave permanent scars when it was all over. She knew she would never be the same if or when it was all over. Briggs hadn't been gone long from dropping her off with Brittany. She'd ate breakfast with Brittany and noticed something different about her. Brittany seemed zoned out and in her own world. Tiffany sat down on the couch with Brittany. She was staring at the wall, but not moving. Tiffany hesitated before saying anything.

"Is everything okay, Brittany? You seem a little off today."

Brittany looked over at Tiffany and smiled.

"I'm okay; I just have a lot on my mind."

Tiffany didn't want to pry, but she felt like Brittany needed to talk it out.

"Want to talk about it? You never know. It might help lift some of it off your shoulders."

Tiffany watched Brittany take a deep breath and look down at her hands.

"Well, there isn't much to talk about. I'm having twins, a boy and a girl. I'm not upset about it. I'm just shocked still I think. I haven't even talked to Michael much about it. He seems okay because I am putting on the face that it's okay. I mean it is going to be okay, but it's just not easy to wrap my head around."

Tiffany couldn't believe that Brittany was going to have twins. She was so happy for them, but she honestly didn't know what to say to her.

"Congratulations on the babies. I know it's hard to take in right now, but look at it this way, you have two bundles of joy to bring home when some people in the world can't even have one."

She noticed Brittany look off in the distance and smiled.

"If it makes you feel any better, I lost my sister's cat."

Brittany stopped smiling. "How did you lose the cat? Was it when the house got broken into?"

"Yeah, it was when the house was broken into. The thing I don't get about the whole break in was they didn't mess with anything but a window. They left a bag of stuff and the front door open. I just want this all over with."

Tiffany thought back to the picture. She couldn't figure out why her mom would want to hurt her own daughters. She wondered for a moment if her mother was even behind everything.

"It will be okay, Tiffany, trust me. It will all work itself out and the guys are working day and night to find the person behind this."

Tiffany knew Brittany was right and the guys were working all the time. She just didn't believe it would be okay. Tiffany and Brittany spent the rest of the day lying around talking. They tried to figure out who the killer was and even had Briggs send over the pictures of the evidence. One minute everything pointed to her mother and the next it just didn't add up. Taylor even joined in on the conversations later that morning.

Tiffany ended up getting a headache and decided to lie down. She called Briggs to let him know she was lying down and would call again when she woke up. It took a long time for her brain to stop working and finally fall asleep. Eventually she drifted off and let her mind rest.

***

Briggs was tired of being on the phone all day and decided to take a break. He pushed his chair away from the desk and folded his hands in his lap. He had been on the phone with different police stations all over the east coast. He tried to track Tiffany's mom, Katie. He thought he had a lead at one point but shortly found out she wasn't there. It was a small town in Kentucky and the police chief remembered arresting someone matching Katie's description. Once they went to the listed address, she was gone, and nothing was left behind. He didn't have high hopes she would be there because it was over two years when she was arrested. The arrest was over something small. Briggs stood up and looked at the clock on the wall. It was six-thirty and he knew Tiffany would want to get home.

He pushed his chair under his desk and turned off his computer screen. He was tired and wanted to get some rest. He turned to walk away and then his desk phone rang. His heart started beating fast as he pulled his chair back out and sat down. He quickly answered the phone, not wanting to miss the call.

"Officer Briggs," he answered.

A woman's soft voice came over the phone.

"Yes, this is Sandra with the Ampster Police Department down here in North Carolina. I was calling because I got the picture of your suspect and I believe she lives in town. She works at a local diner, but I haven't been over there in a few weeks. I can have some detectives ask around and see if they know about her. I can also have her employer pull her file and find out what her address is. I could be wrong but it sure does look like her. Her hair is shorter, and her face has more wrinkles on it, but it looks like her."

Briggs felt something pulling in his gut. He had a feeling Katie was living in that town. He told the woman to hold on the line and went to find Michael. Michael was at his desk with a magnifying glass looking at pictures.

"Hey, I got a call from down in North Carolina saying they have a girl that matches the description of our suspect. She is willing to have people look into it, but I really want to go."

He waited for Michael to say something. Michael jumped up and looked over at Briggs.

"Tell her we are on the way then call Tiffany to let her know we'll be leaving town. We can have Brittany take her home to get some stuff and y'all can stay with us tonight."

Briggs ran off to his desk and got back on the phone. He told Sandra he was coming to investigate and to keep it quiet. He didn't want Katie getting spooked and running off. He hung up the phone and ran to the front of the office to find Michael. He could feel something in his gut telling him he was going to get answers. He only hoped they were the ones he wanted.

CHAPTER TWENTY-THREE

Tiffany woke up to darkness around her. She wondered where she was at first, but soon remembered she was at Brittany's house. She sat up and looked for her phone. She found it on the bed where it must have fallen out of her pocket. She looked at the time and jumped up. It was close to seven o'clock and she noticed she had six missed calls. She swiped her phone open and saw they were all from Briggs. She also had a text from him.

I have to go follow a lead in NC. Brittany will take you to get some stuff to sleep over. I will be back as soon as I can. I talked to Brittany and know you are sleeping. I hope you got some rest. Text or call when you wake up. Love you.

It took her a second to understand what he sent her, because she was so focused on the love part of the text. She read it again and realized he found something. He had a lead and she wanted to know what it was. She dialed his number and waited for him to answer. The call rang three times and went to voicemail. She jumped up and went to find Brittany. She was sitting at the kitchen table playing on her phone.

"Hey, did you talk to Michael or Jason?"

Brittany looked up at her, and said, "Yeah, Briggs called said they got a lead. They won't be back for a while, but I figured when you got up we could go over and get you some clothes."

Tiffany was angry that Briggs didn't answer his phone. She wanted to know what his lead was. She knew not to take it out on Brittany so she let it go. She sat down at the table with her and finally spoke.

"So, let's go get my stuff and maybe Jason will call me back. I really wish I knew what their lead was."

Brittany patted her on the back and got up walking to the door. She followed behind her and tried to cheer up. She just wanted to know he was okay and she wanted to know if they were close to ending everything. She knew better than to get her hopes set too high, but at that point she didn't care. Hope was the only thing she had left and right then she wasn't going to let it go.

***

Briggs drove the truck out of town towards North Carolina. The drive wouldn't take but an hour and a half, but he was anxious to get there and see what he could find. Michael was sitting in the passenger seat staring at some pictures. Briggs knew better than to say anything because when Michael was working, he was focused. Briggs looked down at his GPS on his phone and drove in silence.

Briggs noticed that Tiffany had called him back. He decided to call her back once he got into the next town since Michael had a magnifying glass out and was still focused on the pictures. Finally Briggs couldn't keep quiet anymore.

"I know how you get when people talk while you're working, but you have been staring at that picture for a while. Want to tell me why?"

Michael looked over at him with a confused look on his face.

"I don't know how to explain it, but I think this picture was copied on top of another picture. I can see hints of stuff in the back ground that don't make sense to be there. Right behind Tiffany's mom there is another little girl way back in the darkness. If I didn't have my magnifying glass then I wouldn't have been able to see it. Plus, there is another person standing behind the other little girl. I can't make the face out of either one of them, but I can tell you it's not Tiffany or Jennifer."

Briggs was confused so he pulled over at the next rest stop. He took the picture and the magnifying glass from Michael. He looked at the picture and saw the girl and a figure behind her. Briggs felt his gut pulling at him. He ran the magnifying glass over the rest of the picture. In the dark parts of the picture spaced out all over were letters.

"Hey, grab a pen and write these letters down for me."

Briggs took the magnifying glass and ran it over the letters calling them out for Michael.

"E–M–M–O–R–F–R–E–H–K–O–O–T–U–O–Y–E–N–I–M–S–A–W–E–H–S. Did you get all of them? They are in that order so what does that spell?"

Briggs looked at Michael as he wrote something down. Michael held the paper up for Briggs to see. Briggs slammed the car in drive and raced down the highway. He made a loop and turned back towards home. He had to get to Tiffany before it was too late. He couldn't believe he missed that clue that was right in his face the whole time. He slammed on the gas and drove as fast as he could. Out of the corner of his eye, he could see Michael making a call. He slammed his phone down on the dash when he didn't get an answer.

"Keep trying to get them, Mike. We have to warn them to stay home!"

***

Brittany pulled up to Briggs' house and got out of the

car. She walked with Tiffany to the door, but realized she left her phone in the car.

"Hey Tiffany, I left my phone in the car. Hang on."

She waddled back to the car, but when she got her phone out Tiffany was already inside. She got cold chills down her spine and instantly knew something was off. She looked down at her phone and noticed she missed a call from Michael. Her phone was on silent and she didn't know it. She slid the screen open and dialed his number. He answered the phone on the first ring and she kept looking all around her.

"We just got to Briggs' house and I got to the door, but forgot my phone. When I went back to get it, Tiffany was gone, and I told her to wait on me. Michael, I just know something is wrong."

She listened to Michael instruct her to call 9-1-1 and get in the car. He wanted her to lock the door and get the gun out of the glove box. She did what he said, but felt guilty for leaving Tiffany in the house alone. He demanded she call him right back and said he was about thirty minutes away. She hung up the phone and dialed 9-1-1. She knew she couldn't put her babies at risk and go in the house. She had to sit back and wait, which was killing her. Her friend was inside and Brittany didn't know what was going on.

***

Tiffany thought Brittany was right behind her, but when she walked in the house and the door shut, she knew Brittany wasn't there. Her whole body froze to the spot and she knew someone was inside the house with her. She couldn't force herself to move and she even felt her stomach flipping. She tried to look through the dark, but couldn't see anything. She jumped when she heard someone click something and looked over to see a light flash. The glow of a lighter showed someone's face, but the light went out before she could make out who it was. She saw a red dot moving in the distance and soon smelled smoke. Someone was smoking a cigarette. She didn't know if it was the smoke or her fear that was making her want to throw up.

She couldn't move for fear they would hurt her. She waited in silence for someone to say something. She heard a soft breath blow out smoke and then a harsh laugh.

"Well, hello Tiffany. I sure have missed you over the past few months. Don't even think of running because I will blow your brains out. Come on over and have a seat on the couch in front of me. I want to see your face better. Here, I'll even turn a light on for you."

A dim light turned on in the corner of the living room and a girl's face lit up near it. Tiffany started to sweat and shake. She had no idea what she wanted from her, but she wasn't going to run. A gun was aimed at Tiffany and she knew if she ran the girl would shoot. She began to pray in her head that Brittany was calling for help and Briggs would come for her. She knew better than to think Briggs was coming, because he was far away by then. She took a step towards the living room and the girl smiled. Tiffany knew then that her life was over.

CHAPTER TWENTY-FOUR

Briggs looked over at Michael when his phone rang. It must have been Brittany again. He knew Tiffany was either in the house or someone grabbed her. Michael put the Brittany on speaker phone and he listened in on Michael's conversation.

"Britt, I don't know how we didn't find it sooner. In the picture was a hidden message that was wrote backwards. There was also another picture of a little girl hidden like someone copied the picture over another picture. The words read out, she was mine. You took her from me."

Brittany sucked in a deep breath and said, "So, who is the girl and what have you put together?"

Briggs wasn't sure what Michael would say, but he kept his eyes on the road and his ears open.

"I don't know who the girl is, but if I had to guess I would say she is related to Tiffany. I know it's not Tiffany's mother doing this and I think it's the girl hidden in the picture. Just stay on the phone with me and let me know if you can see anything."

Brittany didn't say anything for a while. Briggs heart picked up speed when he heard Brittany speak.

"There is a light on in the house now. It's not bright, but I can see it light up a window. I only see one shadow by the window now."

Briggs would bet that was Tiffany standing in the light. His mind went to a thousand different places at that moment. He would never forgive himself if something happened to Tiffany. He loved her and had finally found someone to share his life with. He wasn't ready to give that up yet. He pushed the gas down farther and watched the speedometer pick up speed. He needed to get to her and he was only ten minutes away. He wasn't sure how much longer she had, but he was not giving up.

***

Tiffany sat down on the couch across from the girl and waited for her to speak.

"Do you know who I am, Tiffany?"

Tiffany couldn't say anything so she only shook her head. Her heart was thumping so loud she was sure the girl could hear it.

"I'll tell you who I am, but first let me just say how long I've waited to see you again. It's been only a few days, but I haven't spoken to you in many years. You know I followed you for a long time and saw everything that has happened to you. It took a lot out of me not to kill everyone sooner. You look upset that I'm here, but I don't get why. I have done all of this for you, don't you get that?"

Tiffany had no clue what she was talking about and knew something was off about the girl. Tiffany sighed knowing her night was coming to an end.

"That stupid sister slept with your soon to be husband! You didn't talk to her after that for over six years. How messed up does a person have to be to sleep with your sister's soon to be husband? Hey, don't worry. I took care of that bitch for you. At first, I wanted to frame you for her death and it really did almost work. I hated you so much for everything you had that I never did. I got over it quick because I saw how awful your life really was. I did everything for you and it started with Jennifer. See, she is gone, and you don't have to worry about her ever again. Then there was the soon to be husband. What was his name again? Oh, Justin. Yeah, I took care of that sleaze ball too. He was a horrible person who needed to die, Tiffany. He caused you so much pain and I couldn't bear to watch you hurt anymore. Oh, and let's not forget Mother!"

At that point, the girl leaned over closer to Tiffany and grinned really evil.

"Yeah, she was the worst. You know? She left you and Jennifer all alone in this messed up world. She just dropped y'all off and never came back. It's funny now that I think of it because when I killed her she tried to tell me she left y'all so she could come find me. People will say anything to keep you from killing them. People lie, Tiffany. If you lie to me, I'll kill you too. Now back to what I was saying. Oh, do you know who I am now?"

Tiffany felt her body freeze up. She didn't understand anything the girl was saying. She killed her mother, sister, and Justin? She was trying so hard to get her mind to focus, but nothing was working. She shook her head again.

"Well, I guess I could understand why you don't know who I am. You know, seeing as Mother kept me a secret for so long. That was another reason why I killed her. I mean why hide your own daughter from her sisters? She told me in her last breath that I was crazy and that's why she kept me away. HA! Guess she got the last word in after all. Anyway, we have to get going before your Romeo shows up and tries to stop me. I really don't want to kill you Tiffany. I only want to keep you safe. This world isn't safe for you and me. We have to be together. Do you understand that?"

Tiffany couldn't understand anything. She had a sister

that she never knew about. Why would her mom hide that from her and what did this girl have planned for her? She finally found the words to speak.

"So, you're my sister? What is your name? I just don't understand why Mom would keep you from me. Where are we going?"

She had so many questions, but the girl seemed to be getting angry.

"I already said I don't know why she kept us apart. We aren't safe here anymore so we have to go to my place. My name doesn't matter either, but if it makes you feel better it's Samantha. Now get up and let's go. Now!"

Tiffany jumped when the girl yelled at her. She stood up on her feet and walked to the door. She felt the tip of the gun touch her back and her breathing stopped. Just as she was about to reach for the door, she saw headlights shine in the windows.

Samantha grabbed her arm, and said "Shit, they are here!"

She pulled Tiffany's arm and dragged her back to the living room.

"Shit! Shit! Shit! We're trapped now! This is not how I wanted this to end!"

Tiffany felt Samantha let her arm go. It was brief because she grabbed Tiffany again; this time she tightened her grip.

The front door busted open and in came Briggs with a gun aimed at Samantha. Samantha put the gun up to Tiffany's head. Tiffany wanted to scream but she was too afraid to. She looked Briggs in the eyes and prayed she could tell him she loved him again. She didn't want to die. She prayed she would get the chance to spend the rest of her life with him.

***

Briggs looked at Tiffany with the gun to her head. His heart was breaking as he watched tears stream down her face.

"Let Tiffany go and drop the gun. It doesn't have to be this way."

Samantha grabbed Tiffany's hair and pulled.

"It does have to be this way, Detective. I have to keep her safe from everyone. Don't you idiots see how much she has been through? You won't keep her safe. You'll only hurt her like everyone else has. I am the only one who can protect her. So, you drop your gun. I'll kill her to keep her safe if I have to."

Briggs knew he couldn't drop his gun and he wasn't going to take a chance at shooting her because she was moving too much. He decided to try to talk it out with her.

"What is really going on? Who are you and why do you need to protect Tiffany?"

Samantha pulled tighter on Tiffany's hair and she whimpered. He grinded his teeth and waited for her to speak.

"I am her sister, you idiot. Our mother left her and Jennifer without a care in the world. That bitch is dead because of all the pain she caused Tiffany. Then Jennifer slept with Justin so they both had to die! Don't you see that everyone in her life keeps hurting her? I have to save her from it all! I have to keep her safe from everyone! I can't stand back and let anyone else hurt her! I have to take her to a safe place!" Samantha spat as tears flowed from her eyes.

"At first I hated Tiffany because she had it all and I just wanted her dead. I changed my mind soon after I killed Jennifer! I watched them all fuck her over, can't you see that? Don't even try to tell me you will be good to her because you are just like everyone else. No one can keep her safe but me and if you won't let her go with me then I'll kill her to save her. We have to be together. Don't you get that?"

Briggs tried to find the right words to talk her down.

"I get it. Everyone hurts her, but look at Tiffany right now. She is crying and scared. Don't you think this is hurting her just as much? Put the gun down and let's all talk about this. We can get you both help and make this all okay again."

He watched Samantha's eyes grow darker.

"It was never okay in the first place, you idiot! I was left behind by a no-good mother and then she just up and left her other children. She never even told them about me! What kind of mother does that? I never wanted to do everything I have done, but I had no other choice. I can't live without Tiffany and I won't let anyone else have her!"

Briggs took a step towards them and hoped Samantha didn't notice. He wanted to get close to them so he could make a move.

"I get it. It's been hard on you both. I would be upset, too. You just have to make things right. You can't do that if you hurt Tiffany. You can't fix any of this if you hurt her. You can't be together and work on a real relationship if she is hurt. She needs you in her life and I can help you both with that."

Samantha looked down as if she was thinking about what he said. He felt something in the air shift as he watched her look him in the eyes.

"You're right, we have to be together. We have to fix all of this shit. I have to make things right to keep her safe with me. I love her like no one ever will. You couldn't keep her safe, no one could, and now I have to do it myself. I'll make sure we are together. One way or another, we are going to a safe place."

Tiffany looked in his eyes and mouthed the words I love you to him. He knew in that moment he was going to lose Tiffany.

In a flash, Briggs watched the girl pull the gun up to her own head and fire. The bullet went into her head and came out into Tiffany's head. They both hit the floor and Briggs screamed. He ran over to Tiffany, but it was too late. She was gone. He held her in his arms as tears ran down his face. He lost the only thing that had ever mattered to him. She was gone so fast that he couldn't understand anything. Samantha's words already haunting him You couldn't keep her safe, no one could. He looked down at Tiffany and moved the hair from her face. He failed her and he could never forgive himself. He held her in his arms and everything around him went blank. He couldn't save her.

CHAPTER TWENTY-FIVE

Michael stood near a willow tree with Brittany by his side. It was the day Tiffany was laid to rest and put in the ground. Michael spent the past week collecting all the evidence he could to put the pieces together. Briggs shut himself out of the world and Michael understood. Briggs paid for Tiffany's funeral and arranged everything. He took a leave of absence from work and refused to talk to anyone. Michael knew he needed to give him his space so he would leave him alone for the time being.

In the past week, Michael traveled to North Carolina to the last sighting of Katie Childress. He found the house where Katie called home along with Katie's body. She had been stabbed multiple times with the fatal blow being a stab wound to the heart. The house was destroyed, but a note laid next to Katie's body. Michael hadn't told Briggs about the note, but he knew in time he would have to.

The day before the funeral Michael had found the house Samantha was staying at. The owner of the property told Michael that Samantha had been living in that house for nine years. It was a small home in the next town over. It didn't have any furniture in it and she paid in cash. There were pictures tacked to the walls in every room. Michael had never seen anything like it before. She had pictures of Tiffany and Jennifer as children, all the way up to adulthood. Apparently Samantha had been following Tiffany and

Jennifer for many years before ending her life and theirs. In one of the rooms in the house laid a cover and a pillow. In the bathroom Michael found the tools she used to cut up Justin Wilder's body. In a back bedroom, there was a small table with gloves and items Samantha had used to copy Tiffany's finger prints. Michael couldn't get over Samantha using Tiffany's finger prints to frame her.

Michael found Samantha's diary. He was still working on reading through it. Most of the pages he had read were a crazy jumble of words all over the page. She wasn't right in the head and Michael was sure of that. A more thorough investigation of her home was being done and Michael would get the information as it came in.

Michael worked on finding out where Samantha had gotten the gun from, but had no luck. It was a 9mm that she could have purchased off the street anywhere. The gun only had one bullet in it and Michael knew that Samantha had planned to use it on Tiffany and herself no matter what. Michael wanted to let Briggs know that nothing he did would have changed the outcome of Tiffany's death.

Brittany nudged Michael and brought him out of his memory. He looked up and saw a red eyed Briggs walking towards him. Michael saw Briggs' pain all over his face and he knew to tread lightly with what he said. He walked up and hugged Briggs tight. He was hurting for his partner and friend. Briggs pulled back and put his hands in his pockets. He wouldn't make eye contact and Michael figured it was because he was embarrassed and hurting.

"Have you figured out anything new?"

Michael didn't want to answer the question knowing Briggs wasn't ready for answers yet. He knew if he didn't, Briggs would get more upset.

"Yeah, we found a good bit of information, but right now

you should take some time to grieve Briggs."

Briggs looked down at his feet then into Michael's eyes. "I can't grieve until I know what happened and why. I have to know why Tiffany died the way she did. I'll never be at peace until I know."

Michael shook his head and looked off into the distance. The view was beautiful and the weather was finally warming up. The mountains were turning green and the sky was clear that day. He looked back at Briggs.

"Okay, but let's go somewhere else and talk about it. Want to come over to my house?"

Briggs nodded and walked off towards his truck. Michael grabbed Brittany's hand and walked back to their car.

"How is he doing, baby?"

"I don't know babe, but he wants answers and I can't keep them from him." Brittany nodded and got in the car.

After getting home, Brittany grabbed Michael and Briggs a beer and left them to talk in the kitchen. Briggs sat down at the table and Michael sat with him. He had grabbed his laptop from the office just in case Briggs wanted to see any evidence.

Michael took a sip of his beer before he said, "I think it's best if you just ask questions and if I can answer them, I will."

Briggs set his beer down and looked at Michael.

"Okay. Who was Samantha?"

Michael opened his laptop and pulled up Samantha's ID.

"Her name was Samantha Alexis Pinner. She was never married. She was thirty-seven years old and didn't have much family left."

Michael paused before he told him the rest.

"She was Tiffany and Jennifer's half-sister. Her mother was also Katie Childress. Katie had Samantha before Tiffany and Jennifer. She left her behind and never told Tiffany or Jennifer about Samantha."

Michael watched Briggs expression change to anger. Michael wondered if talking to Briggs was a good idea. Soon Briggs' face changed backand he seemed to calm down.

"Did you search Katie's house and what did you find?"

Michael pulled up a picture of Katie's body.

"Katie was struck many times with a knife and the final blow to the heart killed her. The house was trashed, but nothing was missing as far as we know. There was a note by her body and so far, we have matched the writing to hers. We were able to learn a lot from the note and it was addressed to Tiffany and Jennifer."

Michael turned the screen to face Briggs again and showed him the note.

My sweet Tiffany and Jennifer,

I know that no matter what I say it will never be enough. I can never fully explain everything to you in a letter but I hope it helps you both with closure. I always took your father's death harder than I ever wanted to. I never wanted to leave you but I feared I had no other choice. Please understand that what I am going to tell you is a lot to take in but I promise I never meant to hurt either of you.

Before I met your father I was with a man and had my first child. Her name was Samantha. She was so beautiful when she was born and such a great baby. I gave her the world and did my best to raise her. The man I was with was very good to me and Samantha

Ricky (Samantha's father) suddenly passed away. He was in great health and it never made sense. We had an autopsy performed and long story short he was murdered. It took many months of investigating to finally come to an end. Samantha had poisoned her own father at the age of ten. I never noticed the signs that Samantha was in need of help. If I had noticed them, then maybe Ricky would still be alive. I have looked back over the years and see the signs now. From dead animals showing up on our porch to wetting the bed. We even caught her one time trying to smother a baby I was watching for a friend. As a mother, I ignored the signs because I loved Samantha and never wanted to believe something was wrong with her. She needed help and unfortunately I didn't get it for her in time.

Let me fast forward just a little for you both. I admitted Samantha to a psychiatric ward and because she murdered her father she was forced to be there until they thought she was fit to be released. I had to make a really hard decision that day and it was to either keep Samantha or put her up for adoption. I chose to put her up for adoption. I know you may think of me as a monster but please understand that I never wanted to hurt anyone. I only wanted her to get the help she needed, and I knew I could never give that to her. Later in life I met your father and married him. I then had both of you and could rebuild my life with y'all. I from time to time would check on Samantha to see how she was doing. They would never give me much information because she wasn't legally my child anymore. They would only tell me if she was making progress or if she had set backs.

Your father knew about Samantha and encouraged me to check on her as often as I needed. One day when I called to check on her, I was told that she was released from the institution for good behavior and was also developing well with her issues. They assured me she would be monitored and if any changes occurred they would let me know. I first panicked but then I trusted what they told me as far as Samantha doing better. I was happy that she was able to have a shot at a normal life. I never got a call that she was put back in the institution so I went on with my life.

The day your father passed away was a very hard day for us all. I felt something different in my gut, but I refused to follow it at the time. When I asked for an autopsy to be performed on your father, the police refused to have it done and I was told it was not needed. It took some time, but eventually they agreed to go through with it. I had to explain my past with Samantha and that she had been released. After they looked into Ricky's murder, they gave the okay. I know this is all a lot for you at one time, but please give me a chance to explain. I ignored the signs that Samantha needed help once and I didn't want to make that mistake again. I had to listen to my heart and make sure that your father wasn't murdered.

The results came back three weeks later that your father had suffered a heart attack behind the wheel of the car he was driving. The only problem was your father was healthy and never showed signs of heart problems. They performed a toxic screening on your father and it came back with extreme amounts of potassium chloride that had been injected into his body. It caused your father's heart attack and was the key they needed to see that he was murdered. I knew Samantha killed him, but I had no proof and neither did the police. They couldn't find Samantha, but I knew she was close by. The day I found out about your father's murder and Samantha not being found, I decided to leave. I had to leave you both so you would be safe. I knew Samantha was mad at me and not you two and I wanted to keep it that way. I was okay with her trying to kill me, but I could never live with myself if she hurt either of you.

I don't know if I will ever send this note to you because I know how hurt you both must be with me. I promise I never wanted to leave you both, but I had no other choice. I needed you both safe because that was something I couldn't do for Samantha. I love you both with all my heart and I hope you both can forgive me. Know that I have always watched you both from a distance. If I could do it all over, I promise you I would have. I'm here for you both if you need me and I hope Samantha is caught. Once she is caught, I promise to return to see you both. My love will never end for either of you and I promise one day we will be together again. You both are my heart and world.

Love always,

Mom

Briggs looked back at Michael with tears in his eyes.

Michael was hurting for his friend. Briggs looked back to the screen.

"So, Samantha did all this because she was mentally ill? I just don't understand. Why kill Tiffany and Jennifer?"

"Briggs, Samantha had a lot of mental issues and needed help. She learned how to trick the nurses and doctors into thinking she was better. Once she was released from the institution, she went right back to her old ways. She was mad at her mother, but also mad at Tiffany and Jennifer. Think about it, Briggs. As a child Samantha spent most of her life in an institution and when she got out she found out her mother left her and moved on with her life. I know she left Tiffany and Jennifer, but neither of them suffered from mental illness so their prospective wasn't as tragic as Samantha's. I'm sure she obsessed about it during her stay at the institution. Once she was free she stalked Jennifer and Tiffany to find flaws in their lives to justify her rage against them. Jennifer made it easy by sleeping with Tiffany's fiancé; ruining what relationship she and Tiffany had. Samantha thought at first that Tiffany was the perfect one and wanted Tiffany to pay for having the things she couldn't have. That's why at first she tried to frame Tiffany, but somewhere along the way she became obsessed with her instead. Her mind was all over the place. It went from planting finger prints to thinking she could save her from the world. Think about it, Briggs. The only person who didn't have any flaws in her life was Tiffany. She was a great person and Samantha had no reason to kill her. Samantha she thought she could keep Tiffany safe from the world. She thought she could keep her from making flaws in her life. Samantha needed help, but like most cases, the system failed her. There wasn't anything you could have done, Briggs. This isn't your fault and if you go on with your life thinking it is then what would Tiffany think? Please listen to me, Briggs. Take your time and get better. Just don't blame yourself. If you want to blame someone then blame the system for failing Samantha."

Briggs wiped away tears and stood up.

"Thank you for letting me know what all you found. I'm going to talk to the chief and see when I can come back. Sitting at home isn't going to do anything, but drive me crazy. I need to work and keep this off my mind. I do want to ask you and Brittany for a favor and if you say no then it's okay."

Michael nodded and waited for the question.

"Can you both go through all of Tiffany's things? I would like to donate it all to someone. I already got the things I wanted and put them away."

"Of course, we will do that. It might take some time, but don't worry, we got it."

"Thanks man."

Briggs started walking towards the door and Michael followed. They got to the door and Michael closed it behind Briggs as he walked out.

***

Briggs walked in his house and hung his keys up on the hook. He froze in his tracks when he looked at the hook. He smiled a little thinking back to Tiffany. She had bought the hooks a few months prior because she was tired of him losing his keys. He let the memory go and walked past the living room to his bedroom. Since Tiffany died, he hadn't stepped foot in the living room and didn't know if or when he would be able to. He flipped on the light to his room and almost jumped out of his skin.

On his bed was the cat Tiffany had gotten from her sister. He didn't understand how the cat got back inside the house. It had gotten out when Samantha broke into his house and hadn't been back. He felt tears running down his face. He hated the cat, but at that moment he couldn't help but feel like Tiffany sent the cat to him; like she knew he needed a friend. He walked over to the bed and sat beside the cat. It was lying on one Tiffany's shirts that were laid out on the bed. Briggs had slept with one of Tiffany's shirts every night because it smelled like Tiffany. It brought him comfort and helped him get a few hours of sleep each night. He rubbed the cats head and heard it purr. At that moment he couldn't wrap his head around how he could go on in life without Tiffany, but he knew he didn't have a choice. He would just have to cherish the memories they had made over the past year.

FRAMED 3
Preview...

Jessica watched as a car drove past her and blew the horn. It was one of her customers that were unhappy about the service. She was just as mad at him, as he was at her. He wanted a full workout but didn't want to pay the full price. She had been working the streets long enough to know how to deal with guys like him. When he tried to yell at her and grab her, she simply reached over and grabbed his sack with a tight grip. After watching his face change and his attitude go away, she let him go and got out of the car. She didn't have time for that and needed to make some money that night. Jessica was behind on bills, even though that was nothing new, she still had to eat along with everything else. She planned to work over that night and try to make enough so she wouldn't have to be on the street the next night.

She watched as her pimp walked down the street into an alley. She couldn't stand him but he did keep her safe when she needed it. She pulled out her phone and looked at the time. It was two o'clock in the morning and she only made a hundred dollars. After her pimp got his cut she would go home with around sixty dollars; not enough to pay off any of the bills she needed to. She turned and walked down the next street hoping someone stopped because if the night kept going the way it was, she would be back there the next night.

Jessica knew her outfit was on point that night and most men wouldn't be able to resist her. She had her low-cut black tank top on and a pearl white leather skirt that just about showed her goods. She traveled light and only kept a black clutch with her. Her heels were a good six inches and shiny black. Summer in Tennessee were brutal so she wore as little as she could and not to mention for easy access.

Just as Jessica turned on the street a car slowed down beside her. She turned to face the lights shining in her face. She waited for the car to stop and bent down to the open window. She waited for the guy to speak but when he didn't she figured he was shy.

"Are you looking for some company tonight baby?"

She couldn't see his face well but she could tell he had big arms because his hands clutched the steering wheel tight. Jessica waited patiently for him to respond. He finally answered in a deep tone.

"Sure get in."

She didn't hesitate and jumped in the car. She shut the door and looked over at him.

"So, do you wanna do it here or do you have a place? If I leave it does cost a little more but I'll make it worth it," she said as she reached her hand over and rubbed his leg.

She smiled when she heard him moan a little.

"I have a place and don't worry price isn't a problem."

She loved the sound of that and buckled her seat belt. They rode in silence but she kept rubbing all over him. She wanted to make his night good in hopes of him paying her good. If she was lucky he would pay her enough that she wouldn't have to work the next night. She made a mental note to up her price seeing that he didn't mind paying.

Jessica started to wonder where they were going when she realized the ride was taking a long time. It had been almost forty minutes and they were on a back road.

"Hey how much longer until we get there, baby? I don't wanna go too far because I have to work tonight. I mean if you want me for the whole night it will be kinda pricy."

He turned to her smiled and said, "I told you I don't mind the price. I'll take the whole night charge and even give a good tip."

She started to get excited and figured for the first time in a long time she might enjoy herself for once. Jessica never liked working and hated almost all her clients. This guy was different. She hoped that if he liked what she was giving then maybe he would be a repeat customer. She wasn't going to push it through because she was just happy at how much she was going to make.

Thirty more minutes into the ride and she finally saw a gas station ahead. He pulled into the gas station and parked at the gas pumps. "I need to get some gas that way I don't have to stop in the morning on our way back. Do you want anything?"

She was happy he had asked because she was both hungry and thirsty.

"Sure, can you grab me a honey bun and a water?"

He nodded and got out of the car. She watched him walk to the counter with some stuff in his hands. It didn't take him long and he was walking back to the car. After pumping gas, he jumped in the car and they were off again. That time the trip only lasted fifteen minutes. He pulled into an apartment complex and shut off the car. She got out of the car when he did and followed him into the building. He turned and went into the first door on the left side.

The apartment was nice. She could immediately tell he had money. Jessica followed him through the kitchen and into the living room. She looked over at him and couldn't help but wonder why he needed a prostitute. He was really good looking and could easily get a girl with no questions asked. She shrugged it off because she didn't get paid to ask questions. She watched him walk to her and stop about a foot from her. She looked up at him which was surprising because even in six-inch heels he was a good two foot taller than her. She wrapped her hands around his body.

He pulled them off of him and said, "Let's go to my room to do this okay?"

Jessica smiled and eagerly followed him. Once in his room she didn't pay much attention to anything around her. She only noticed the bed and some rope near the night stand. He pulled her shirt off. She didn't object to it and soon all her clothes were off and on the floor. He stood and looked at her but she didn't mind. It was his money so she would let him spend it any way he wanted to.

He pushed her on the bed hard and it almost knocked the wind out of her. She was so shocked by it that she didn't know what to do or say. He jumped on top of her and his face was only a few inches from hers. He smiled at her and she felt a cold chill run down her back. Her stomach started to hurt and her heart was beating fast. He grabbed her hands and put them over her head in one swift move. He held them in place above her head with one hand. With his other hand, he reached in his pocket and before she knew it a rag was over her face and darkness followed soon after.

When Jessica woke up she felt her head pounding and the room was spinning. It was dark in the room but a small light was glowing in one corner. It was quiet and at first, she didn't know where she was. She tried to move her legs and arms but they wouldn't move. She looked up to her arms and saw them tied down to the bed. . She started to panic when she realized her legs were tied down as well.

"Someone help me!"

Her mind was racing and she was so scared.

"No one can hear you," came from the corner of the room.

She kept screaming and prayed he was lying. He walked over to the bed and tears ran down her face.

"Please don't do this to me. I'll walk all the way home and I won't tell anyone anything."

He never said a word and she knew in her heart he was going to rape her. He had a cup in his hand and she was scared to see what was in it. He walked to her feet at the end of the bed and looked up at her.

"This is going to hurt but it's worth it remember? Isn't that what you said to me? It's worth it!"

She watched in horror as a clear liquid poured slowly out of the cup and onto her foot. It instantly started to burn. She started to scream as the pain ran up her foot to her leg. He kept pouring until he got her hip. She watched her flesh melt and blood poured out of her body. She kept screaming hoping someone would hear her. She felt dizzy and prayed for God to take her. She was wrong about being raped. He was going to kill her. He repeated the process to the other leg and Jessica started to fade in and out. The pain was going away and she knew she was dying. He walked up to her face with the cup in his hand.

"It was worth it, wasn't it?"

Those words were the last thing she heard as he poured the liquid over her face. She screamed in horror. Seconds later darkness came over her and Jessica took her last breath.

ACKNOWLEDGMENTS

I would like to give a big thanks to all my fans for all the support I received after writing my first book Framed. I feel myself developing so much from all the feedback y'all are giving me. I pray to continue to write for you in many genres. I love you all and thank you again.

I want to give a big thanks to my aunt Jan Shaw. She has been a major fan from day one and has kept me on track when I couldn't focus. She is such an encouraging person with a beautiful attitude on life. Thank you, Jan, for believing in me and going on this journey with me.

Another thank you to my beautiful mother and father. Through good times and bad you have made me look at life in another way. I can feel me growing as a person because of you both. I love you both so much.

Also thank you to my wonderful fiancé, Michael Rio. I haven't seen someone support anyone the way you do me. I have wanted to give up before but you pushed me to keep going. You are mine and our families rock. You and our three children have made my life complete. Thank you for always being there no matter what. I love you so much.

Finally, I want to thank my beautiful and smart publisher Sharon Seigler. You have shown me so many things in these past few months. I have been able to grow and learn so much from you. You are an amazing teacher and have been so patient with me through this process. I couldn't ever thank you enough for all you have done. You believed in me from the start and gave me the chance of a lifetime. Thank you for allowing me to be great through you.